INFINITE SUMMER
Poolside Reader

Created in partnership with WBS Apparel

The British at Tortola
@LarmusTafil2929

On July 2nd, 1672, the British galleon was anchored by her trusty crew outside the pretty, little Caribbean Island of Tortola. Right as the anchor plunged past the clear water, Colonel William Burt called her crew onto the deck. It was to be them to seize the island from the Dutch by landing ashore and securing a beachhead.

The square faced, English colonel shouted at his crew, "Line up then! Line up there! Easy now! Do not go on making a fool out of our King!"

The twenty or so chosen swashbucklers lined up as straight as they could before their colonel. Their legs swayed like branches in the wind, their faces were red from being out in the sun and from the gallons of beer that was onboard that were common rations for the boys. One fellow at the end of the line had a wooden pail in his hand and he raised it to his lips.

"Albert!" shouted the Colonel, his square face bursting red. "You lazy fool! Put that down!"

The sailor dropped the empty pail onto the ground, saluted and said, "Aye, aye captain'!" Then the fool leaned back to the point where he flopped onto the ground, passing out.

"Ah, devil take him! Go on, lower the rowing boats! Pack some guns before we row ashore! Move!"

The nineteen selected sailors moved about haphazardly, arming themselves with cutlasses and matchlocks. Burt readied himself by going into his quarters and relieving his thirst by helping himself with a bucket of beer. All the men, hustling about broke out into a simple rhyme:

> *All the pretty ladies we shall touch*
> *And there won't be ever too much!*
> *As we'll raise our voices with cheers*
> *'Cause it's us with the buckets of beers!*

The first rowboat was a disaster, as the sailors were meant to cut the ropes at the same time. Instead, the boat dangled, with the bow up in the air and then dropped into the water only to capsize. One drunken sailor jumped overboard into the warm water, managed to right the boat and hopped aboard. They all whooped, having just saved the expedition to Tortola. To celebrate a bucket or two of beer were passed among the boys, taking hearty gulps. The sailor down in the water demanded a share, but when they dropped the pail, they missed, with it falling wide and its yellow liquid mixing with the clear water of the Caribbean.

"Oh, damn it all!" cried the sailor as he fruitlessly tried scooping up water with his hands.

Back on the deck, the rest managed to drop the second rowboat without issue. One by one, they slid down ropes onto the boats, evenly spread out with ten folks on either one. The last aboard was the colonel with a lit tobacco pipe dangling from his lips.

"Row us to shore, boys!" he cried.

They rowed from the anchored galleon to the beach of Tortola. The sun was cooking them, but they cared not in the slightest. Some of the men realized they ought to load the guns, just in case, and tend to the lit matches. Each of the waves were gentle, making for a rather easy journey. Burt was sitting down with a small smile slowly growing on his face.

Before long, the boats were rammed ashore. They all piled out at the same time, one fellow was off balance and fell back first onto the shallow beach. Warm water of a wave soaked him before the colonel managed to help him up. A drunken hiccup escaped both, at the same time. The group pulled both boats further ashore, to stop them from drifting out back to sea.

When they finished, Burt collected them into a pile. "For a couple of drunken Englishmen, I'd say we've done our King proud!"

The rest cheered, "Hurrah for the Colonel and King!" Without direct orders, the fellows had brought a massive pail, so large and filled with beer that it took two men to carry it by the handle. They dropped it so they could partake in their impromptu celebration.

While they cheered, just past the beach on the edge of the jungle, three Dutchmen, one armed with a matchlock musket, looked on. The one with the gun whispered to the other two, "*We hebben een serieus probleem: de Engelsen zijn hier.*"

Having realized this, two of the Dutchmen fled back across the island, to their island fort. The last fellow raised his gun, aimed at the group and fired. Smoke bellowed from the barrel with a roar. The bullet flew in the open air, smashing right into the massive pail and coming out the other end. A wave of yelps erupted from the sudden fire.

Only seven Englishmen had guns, but they all returned fire, aiming toward the smoke in the jungle line. The lurking Dutchman had already fled, leaving the sailors alone on the shore. They looked down at the leaking bucket which had already been emptied. All the men sighed with dissatisfaction. They turned to their colonel.

Burt replied, tobacco pipe still dangling, "By mid-July, my God, we shall have 'em licked right and proper. Hail the crew back aboard for more supplies and in time we'll have this slice of tropical paradise for ourselves."

Hammerheads
@BobWills64

When you live in Wisconsin where do you go for summer vacation? Answer: Wisconsin. It is well known that true Wisconsin aristocrats go to the Northwoods to have "fun." But vacations in the Northwoods aren't mere fun – they're survival!

The aristocratic crew I run with call themselves the Hammerheads. We are true sons of Wisconsin. After a Hammerhead survival-vacation you don't feel rejuvenated, you feel depleted. You may feel rejuvenated days later, but on Monday you will likely experience physical convulsions and existential crises. When you gaze into the Northwoods Abyss, the Northwoods Abyss gazes back into you.

The Hammerhead survivacation consists of: sun burns (sunscreen is forbidden), cheap liquor (the more difficult the brand is to pronounce the better), tobacco in all forms, maybe some contraband, mosquitoes, ticks, chiggers, water-skiing, bonfires, hammocks (not for relaxing, but for sleeping on, in the cold, with the mosquitoes), dudes sleeping on the floor next to open couches, dudes sleeping on beds together, dudes sharing cigarettes, a game called washers (alternatively "warshers"), bald eagles and balding men, loons and lunatics, cold water and warm beer.

By day, the Hammerheads have legitimate careers and good reputations (some even have wives!), but on survivacation, they shapeshift into werewolves. Doctors smoke cigarettes, firefighters start bonfires with gasoline, professors expose themselves, and business owners trip on psychedelic mushrooms. All types of neighbors and other assorted characters stop by, either on boat or ATV, and every one of them is a personality. Guys by the name of: Johnny Muscle, Chung Balls (don't ask me), Redman, Yitty from the City, Skut (a.k.a. Skunt), Cocktail Willy, and The Commodore. The Wisconsin accents get thicker, the language verges on the blasphemous, and the laughter becomes maniacal.

Homebase is Lac du Flambeau, but the Hammerheads also haunt Minocqua, Tomahawk, Upson, Hurley, and Mercer. During the summer, on Saturdays, the town of Tomahawk puts on a water- ski show. Water-skiing is a big part of Northwoods culture and tradition. The whole town comes out to enjoy the evening. Grandparents and grandchildren, families sitting on blankets.

The Hammerheads have been coming to the ski show for years, some of them since they were little kids themselves. They know the history and lore of the ski show and all kinds of esoterica surrounding it. The ski show is pretty tame these days but there are legends of a skier years ago who would wear a kite, and as the boat accelerated, he was lifted out of the water and into the air. Well, the Hammerheads knew about this guy, and they made it their mission to coax him out of retirement. It was kind of like Batman in The Dark Knight Returns, or some Clint Eastwood movie where the townspeople beg and plead with the ol' gunslinger to save everyone from the bad guys one last time.

The Hammerheads took their seats in the stands and immediately started yelling out one-liners, non-sequiturs, hilarious quips, and inside-references only other Hammerheads would understand. They started yelling they wanted to see the old-time classic skiers from back in the day: Ronny Kaplonic, expert with the slalom ski, Mean Gene, the guy who would wear the kite, a mythical skier by the name of 'Roid Belly (no idea), and the boat driver, the man with the perfect archetypal Wisconsin name, Mike Hilgendorf.

There was actually an MC for the show, on microphone, and he took all the yelling in stride. After a while, he opened it up to the entire crowd for questions. Immediately, eight arms shot up from the Hammerheads like they were in 3rd grade again – "oooh, oooh, oooh, question! question! question!" I don't know what the hell the MC was thinking, but the crowd seemed to love it. The Hammerheads quickly took over and became the show within the show. Imagine a press conference full of retards. We assaulted that poor MC with ridiculous minutiae and time-wasting questions about the specs of the boat and the specs of the motor. We asked if Mike Hilgendorf imagines his arm as an extension of the boat – man and machine perfectly integrated. We asked what the latest was on Ronny Kaplonic. And we asked if Gene would come out of retirement to fly once more. The crowd was laughing hysterically, probably wondering how we knew everyone by name, but the Hammerheads know about everything that goes on in Northern Wisconsin.

The MC seemed to want to avoid questions about Gene, as if those days were over, and Gene didn't water-ski anymore. But the Hammerheads persisted, and out of the mist walked Mean Gene for one last ride! The Hammerheads cheered and roared! Gene returned to water-ski into the night sky like a majestic eagle one last time. Gene got in the water, Hilgendorf fired up the boat, took a few warm-ups, then gunned it with machinic precision. Gene soared into the horizon and nearly decapitated himself on the highway bridge.

Pure Wisconsin magic.

As I said, the aftermath of a Hammerhead survivacation brings on existential crises and revaluations of all values. Your skin is sunburn red, your body is sore from water-skiing, you probably have to dig bugs out of your hair, you started drinking at 9AM for the past three days, you didn't eat all day, you gorged yourself at 1AM, then you puked it back up while laying by a sweltering fire, your mouth is scarred from chew, your throat hurts from all the cigarettes, your urine is orange, you got into fights, you negotiated fights, every terrible detail of your past was brought up and laughed at, and all you have to look forward to is a four-hour car ride home. You are truly pathetic and worthless. All you want is mommy. You beg for mercy. You'll be lucky if you can manage to bang your girlfriend Sunday evening. You swear you'll never come back up here. Drinkers pledge sobriety, playboys consider marriage, and atheists become believers.

To the Hammerheads: Guardians of the Wisconsin Northwoods!

Tubing
Dr. John T. Parce

My bros and I wake up early on Saturday. My head's pounding, we were celebrating the end of the semester up until about three hours ago, but nothing's stopping us. Junior year's over. I have a precious few days before I'm expected back home in Corpus to work at my dad's shop. The guys all say they'll come down next weekend so we can hit the beach. But today is about tubing.

We throw on swim trunks and tank tops. The tubes go in the back of Tim's RAV4 and then we fill the coolers. After the fuck-up with the big cooler last year, we came around to getting a few of those personal-sized inflatable ones.

We get creative with the booze because cans and bottles are banned at the Guadalupe. I pour a couple fingers of whiskey into a CamelBak bottle and brim it with Coke. The bros used to make fun of me for the frozen pre-mixed margaritas and fuzzy navels but I've made believers out of them. Packs of beef jerky and a ziplock bag with smokes and a lighter go on top.

The drive takes two hours. It's hot by the time we get to New Braunfels. We blow up our tubes while we stand in line for the bus to the river entrance. The heat radiates off the pavement and the bus smells like diesel. But the water in the Guadalupe is always cold. Looking forward to that.

Since we have our own tubes, we skip the rental line. But we get a locker to hold our phones and stuff. I lash the tube and cooler together and get cozy. Headache disappears instantly. I lay back and put my hat over my face. I think about how the water particles move together for a short time and then disperse into the environment.

A bump. I sit up in my tube. I'm at the traffic jam before the first chute. I was out for about forty-five minutes. I can't see any of my bros. That doesn't bother me. This float has a designated start and stop.

Things open out after the chute. I drag my stuff up the concrete steps to the first rest stop, with the picnic tables, wondering if the bros are waiting here. They're not. I sit down and dig my smokes out. She asks if she can have one.

I look up. She's my age, cute face, dirty-blonde hair cut above her shoulders. Can't help but notice her body in her olive-green bikini. I slide a couple of cigarettes out of the pack and tell her one of them is hers if she sits down. She does. I light up and tell her my name. She says hers is Alison.

I ask what she's doing here alone. She says she lost her friends and she feels dumb for not bringing her phone. She doesn't trust those waterproof carriers they sell. I don't either. She's eyeing my cooler and I can tell she's thirsty. I tell her to help herself. When she reaches down, I see a tattoo of the back half of an arrow, as if it's pierced between her shoulder blades.

"Oh, my God," she says. "A fuzzy navel?"

I tell her she's welcome to it. I pick up the CamelBak bottle. It's gotten a little bit warm because this cooler doesn't actually insulate for shit and when I open the nozzle a jet of foam shoots straight up in the air and she laughs. We drink and share a bag of jerky. She's ready to look for her friends. So am I.

We tie our tubes together. She drinks my booze and shares my smokes and I tell her she's running up a tab. Things get a little blurry after that. At this part of the river, everyone's buzzed. It's noisier, but everyone's having fun.

I catch a prickly and piney smell and I ask loudly who's puffing and not passing. People laugh. Someone's got a speaker and Alison and I sing along to "Drive" by Incubus. A dude is standing up on his tube and throwing cherries at people out of a Tupperware. I catch one and I give it to her. She says it's been soaked in Everclear.

At the second rest stop we lay on the grass. She wants to give me her number. There's a bicycle cop with a pen and notepad. Alison's handwriting's going out the window. Mine would be, too. I stick the paper in the cooler. A distant thought tells me to put it in the bag with the smokes, but it will be fine.

I'm past buzzed when we get back in the water. We wade out chest-deep and I have one hand on our tubes and the other around her waist and I stop to kiss her. I lift her up. She weighs nothing in the river. The Guadalupe is always cold but I still remember the smooth warmth of her thighs around my waist.

My tingling fingertips run along her back under the strap of her top and I ask her why she has an arrow tattoo. She tells me when you get shot with an arrow, the worst thing you can do is pull it back out and you have to push it all the way through. She doesn't elaborate. We hold hands the rest of the way.

At the exit, she finds her friends and tells me goodbye. I promise to text her. I look for the bros but they arrive after me and I realize we probably passed them up at the second rest stop. I empty the cooler of trash and find the paper reduced to pulp, no digits recognizable. I never see her again.

I have an incredible summer. But I think a lot about how she and I, two drops of water, moved together down the river for a moment.

And the Guadalupe is always cold.

AMERICA'S FINEST CLOTHING BRAND

THIS SHIT WILL GET YOU LAID!

- BILLIONS MUST BUY!
- VERY FEW PEOPLE HURT IN THE MANUFACTURING PROCESS.

all you need at:
www.wbsapparel.com
@WBSApparel

The Sundae Kid
Oz

Jacob Sheppard wore a large leather jacket in the hot summer heat. He was boiling but he needed it to conceal his father's pistol, tucked into the waistband of his jeans. He had been careful not to wake his little brother, Joseph, when he left his father's house, as he did not want him around when he went through with his plan. This plan was for him to use his father's gun to steal an ice cream truck. He would drive his friends around along with Lucy Warden. Then he would drive with everyone to somewhere, anywhere, and they would have ice cream and soda along with a refrigerated car to enjoy all day. Then one by one everyone would leave for the night, Jacob and Lucy were alone. Then he would kiss her goodnight. The faint music of a distant ice cream truck tore Jacob from his vision. He picked up his head and his pace, like a bloodhound on a thief's tail. With any hope he would catch up to the truck while it was serving some customers. The music of the truck grew louder and louder as Jacob wove through the side streets and alleys. When the music was at its loudest, Jacob saw it, a large white truck with sun-discolored painted-on pink, yellow and blue bubbles. This faded whimsicality that served as a prelude to Jacob's premeditated violence would have tickled his sense of irony if he had one. Three children waited in line, each clutching dollar bills soaked by their sweaty palms. He waited till the last child made his way down the sidewalk with his ice cream before he approached the service window.

"Well hello there young man, what can I get you?" The man's black appraising eyes did not notice Jacob's nervous demeanor as he approached the window.

"I'll take the whole truck."

"You want to buy everything from me? Are you sure I can afford it?" The man's mustache twitched with a patronizing grin. Jacob remembered that he should probably use the gun. He quickly pulled it out of his jeans and pointed it at the driver.

"No, I am not gonna pay one cent, get out the truck, leave the ice cream and the money and give me the keys. Unless you want me to shoot you."

The man's grin melted under the heat of Jacob's threat. He opened his mouth to speak

but nothing came to him and he shut it again. The man raised his arms above his head and obeyed. Jacob drove away with adrenaline drowning out the truck's loudspeakers. When he had driven down three or four blocks, his mind became clear again and he turned off the annoying tune. He would now take his ill-gotten gains to the gang's hideout, an abandoned movie theater. In there would be Sam Barns, and Toby Jackson. Jacob honked the ice cream truck's horn as he waited by the theater's entrance. Sam and Toby ran out to see Jacob sitting in the truck, an inebriated grin on face. He had gotten over his nerves and now he felt the intoxication of conquest and victory.

"How did ya get that Jake?" Sam looked over the truck as he approached, taking in the dingy truck transformed by larceny.

"I took my Papa's gun and hijacked it, that's what." Jacob accentuated his words with a flourish of the gun.

"Is that real?" Sam tried to grab the gun out of Jacob's hand.

"Of course it's real, do you think I'd be able to do this with a toy?"

"Does it have any ice cream?" Toby looked around for another way to enter the truck.

"Yeah, it's got soda too." Jacob pointed to the back of the truck with the gun. "Open up the back and get in. We're gonna go for a drive."

Once everyone was in the truck and they got to work sorting through the freezers Jacob started to drive to Lucy's house. Soon they all had ice cream cones and Coca-Cola bottles in their hands. Jacob only had a drink. He had grown thirsty after the adrenaline wore off. He mulled over what he would say when he arrived. In no time at all he pulled in front of her house. He put the gun on the dashboard and walked up to Lucy's door. He knocked and waited. The door opened and there was Lucy. She was the prettiest girl Jacob had ever seen, wearing a blue gingham dress, matching ribbons that tied her blonde hair into a pair of twin tails.

"Hi Lucy. I drove over here and I was wondering. If you'd want to come with me?"

"Come with you? In what?"

"In that." Jacob gestured to the ice cream truck behind him.

"The ice cream truck? How'd you get that?"

"Stole it."

"You stole it? So you're a felon?" Lucy crossed her arms and glowered at Jacob.

"Felon? No. I never hurt anyone, and I've never been caught and I've never gone to jail."

"That's what a felon is." Jacob shifted under her gaze.

"Like your daddy? I heard he's in jail."

"I am not a felon! Didn't I just say." Jacob felt his face grow red. He hated his father.

"Look can't yo-"

Lucy slapped Jacob, sending him backwards to the ground in surprise. "Get out, I won't have anything to do with any felon! You hear? Now leave!" Lucy slammed the door behind her. Jacob rubbed his stinging face and went back to the truck. It was empty. The gang had left, the gun was gone, and there were only a few bottles and popsicles in the freezers. He wiped the tears from his eyes and he remembered Joseph. Jacob hadn't thought about him once. He would go back and give Joseph all of the popsicles and soda he wanted. Jacob drove home, guided by a bright light that he could not take out of his eyes.

White Boy Summer Lives Eternal
Kris Aldag

ALL HAIL WHITE BOY SUMMER. Every white boy in America, regardless of race, has been called upon to do his Duty. In Atlanta, GA, Prineville, OR, Northern Virginia, etc., server-rack exhaust fans work overtime to dissipate the heat generated by thousands upon thousands of posts proclaiming the beginning of White Boy Summer. Anticipation has replaced apprehension and the prospects of a better tomorrow echo in hearts all across America. I will not be a mere observer, because, above all, White Boy Summer can only exist through the actions of its many participants.

It's morning on the first day of White Boy Summer (White Boy Summer doesn't have an objective start date — it begins when the feeling surges through you and grabs you by the throat). I wake up, and a minute later, my phone's blue-light glow lights up my face.

I open X, and swipe to the "For You" tab. Another account announces the beginning of White Boy Summer. My motions are automatic, like every morning. Today: Press repost. Look at another post, from a big account. It asks, what is the meaning of White Boy Summer? I type out a reply, trying to best use the 280-character limit. The reply goes over — should I abbreviate White Boy Summer to WBS, or would that take something away from my post? I decide to cut some characters elsewhere in the replay, then press post. A notification, a text from my sister, slides onto the screen. I get a courtesy like for my reply, followed by another like 10 minutes later. My account is a small one, but it is always growing. I brush my teeth, shower, grab lunch from the fridge, then leave the apartment for work.

***

You can feel the electricity of White Boy Summer. The feeling is mirrored by the electric hum of the power lines outside, buzzing louder because of the summer heat and synchronizing in an electromagnetic chorus. We all exist at various points in this (spiritual?) power grid. Something big is going to happen. I know it. We're all going to make it.

My phone vibrates. It's my sister. I tell my boss that I'm going to step outside to take the call. My sister needs me to drive five hours to Houston to help her move. Why? Does she not have friends in town? I say maybe. We both know I mean no. I hang up. I take a second to look at the horizon, shimmering because of the 100-degree temperature outside. The heat no longer feels warm and inviting like before — just oppressive.

***

White Boy Summer goes beyond the internet. It is a mindset. It isn't just posting memes, sharing videos, et al. It's a call to action, to Become Who You Are. It's an arbitrary date that nevertheless provides the catalyst for a big change, like picking the first day of the month to kick a bad habit, or waiting for a holiday to start hitting the gym. I get home. I pull my phone out of my back pocket as I walk toward the couch, getting ready to sit down. After work, it's necessary to decompress. Swipe up, enter the passcode, pick an app.

Time stops in the phone's infinite scroll. If you can't do something tangible, then suspending time is an acceptable alternative.

(White Boy Summer is real, but not something totally offline. It's about all of us, and it's not like you can ask a random guy on the street and ask him how his White Boy Summer is going.)

Inside the infinite scroll, there are no outside events to mark the passage of time. There is only me, projected outward, everywhere into the digital world (now just the world). Something I posted in the afternoon blows past my usual number of likes, mostly from accounts I don't know. I see a text from my sister — nothing about the move, just asking about dad. Had I heard from him? She wasn't sure if he was sick or something else. I didn't know, but I'm sure he was fine. I make a mental note to text him tomorrow morning.

***

I was a sophomore in high school and it was a summer like any other, except my mom had died the month before. Dad was despondent but still went in to work Monday through Friday, except he didn't talk as much, not that he talked much before. I remember thinking that my sister was acting overdramatic at the time. She got out of a few final exams, but not all of them. Travis and Zack knocked on my door to invite me out. It was just past noon, and the sidewalk concrete radiated heat. None of us talked about my mom. We walked for three hours. The houses seemed to stretch on forever, broken up by parks, elementary schools and the occasional gas station. We went to Travis' house, then played video games until 11 or 12 p.m., well after my old curfew, before everything happened. I walked the three blocks home, and saw my dad and sister watching something on TV — I didn't know what. I couldn't see their facial expressions, not really, but they invited me to take a seat on the couch.

***

It's the next day and I don't know why, but I depart for Houston, leaving town through rush-hour gridlock, then eventually entering Houston city limits, the city's manageable nighttime traffic illuminated by LED lamplight. I make it to my sister's apartment complex, walk upstairs to her front door, and knock. She opens the door. I had texted her when I left, but she still looks surprised. Small boxes are clustered in her living room, seemingly at random. "I didn't expect to see you," she says Her face tenses up, stressed by the disorder in her apartment or maybe the late hour. She relaxes.

"Did you eat anything on the drive in?"

"No, not really," I reply.

She smiles. "Let's get something to eat."

Coven of the Fireflies
Sean Shaffer

Tonight was going to be one of his last nights in his old neighborhood before he would be heading off to college. The hot summer evening was transforming into a cool night, one haunted by the specter of autumn. Growing up here, such an evening was a dime a dozen. John Antos watched as fireflies danced on his front lawn. The males blinked their affections to the females. Signaling their desire for a mate. Despite the peaceful scene, John was not at peace. A sense of dread had come upon him. John was about to attempt something he had long since feared, he was going to ask his friend, Elizabeth Kendle on a date.

As he drove to her house, The ritual played out in his head, a scene of him asking Elizabeth out. Each idea that came to him felt more cringe than the last. He remembered the last time he saw her. She was with her mom at the grocery store. He walked up to her and said hi. He remembered her pale face, framed by long brown hair. She was wearing a black oversized hoodie. It had an indecipherable metal band logo on it. They talked for a few minutes, but Elizabeth seemed distant, as if her mind was somewhere else.

As he pulled up to her house, John noticed that there were no cars in the driveway. "Perfect," he thought, "Her mother must be out." When he got out of the car, he noticed the front door was already open. Curious, John approached cautiously and looked inside. The front hall was dark, the house was silent. Elizabeth must have gone too. Disappointed, he turned to leave but noticed a faint yellow light coming from further inside the house. Something about that light made his skin crawl. Moving further into the house, he entered into the dining room, where the yellow light was coming from. On the dining room table was a rabbit that had been hacked to pieces. Surrounding the corpse was a circle of black candles; their faint yellow light illuminating the pentagram drawn on the surface of the table. The candles flickered as a cold breeze blew through the open back door.

He found the flashlight on his key chain and moved to the edge of the forest behind Elizabeth's house. John knew that she was probably out there. It was dark but the fireflies illuminated the tree trunks. John picked up a solid looking tree branch before he followed several footprints that led into the forest. Soon a yellow glow appeared in the distance. He turned off his flashlight and approached the light. A ring of candles illuminated the clearing. John observed three black robed individuals standing around a fourth one laying on the ground. As he creeped closer he heard them chanting in some strange language.. The central figure of the three lifted his arms into the air as if to beseech the sky and shouted.

"O tenebrosum, o formidolosum! Offerimus hoc vassallus."

The air around John grew cold, as if he had stepped in front of an open freezer. The candles around the robed figures were snuffed out simultaneously, but John couldn't feel any wind blowing. The central figure started to levitate, long hair reaching downward as if it was trying to keep her from floating away. It was then that John found who he was looking for. Elizabeth's pale face glowed in the moonlight interrupted by a dark stain that covered her mouth and neck. John didn't know what was going on but he knew it wasn't good. He clenched his branch in his hands and charged the nearest robed figure. The branch hammered against his head, sending him to the ground.

"What the hell?" Yelled the robed figure.

John pressed on with his attack before the other two could react. The branch arched down and hit the shoulder of the smallest of the three figures. With a crack both the branch and something else broke. John's victim let out a squeal of pain, she dropped to her knees clutching her shoulder. John's fist connected with the side of her head and sent her sprawling to the ground. The last one reached into his robes and produced a knife stained with blood. It was at this moment John got a good look at his face. John identified him as Fred Cohen, a classmate who would spend his weekends hanging in graveyards and making hacky emo music. Fred took a step forward with a look that made it clear to John that talking was out of the question. Fred lunged, and the blade grazed John, cutting his shirt. Such a clumsy cut, gave John the opening to punch Fred square in the face. Fred stumbled backwards, dropping the knife. John tackled him to the ground and slammed his fists into Fred's greasy face until he stopped moving.

John stood up and turned his attention to Elizabeth who had dropped to the ground while all of this was happening. He put his jacket over her and checked her pulse. She was still breathing. The blood on her mouth and neck looked like it was smeared on rather than from any cuts. He lifted her up and began carrying her to his car. He placed her in the passenger seat and began driving her to the hospital. They had driven a good mile when Elizabeth opened her eyes. She looked about and saw John.

"Don't worry Elizabeth, I'm taking you to the hospital."

Her hand reached over grasping his forearm. "I don't need a doctor, I need a priest." He looked back at her, her eyes were welling with tears,

"John, please."

He nodded, turning the car around. John carried Elizabeth inside the church and they rested in front of the altar. The next morning Father Kevin walked into the asp of the church to find two figures at the foot of the altar. John and Elizabeth lay there asleep with their hands intertwined.

Of Watermelons and Dreamsicles
John Bowman

    The rock flies down the path and stirs up gravelly dust as it lands atop a mound of pebbles. I rub my fingers across the last two smooth stones I have tucked away in the palm of my hand as I kick another down the path. They're cool to the touch just like the sudden nighttime breeze that flows through my hair.

    What should've been a gentle breeze quickly turns into a wind that rustles the bushes to my side and sends the overhead tree branches flapping. The picnic basket draped over my arm snags on a severely overgrown bush and I stumble forward as I yank it free.

    My watermelon slices land right smack in the middle of a heap of dirt, but the hot dogs land on a clump of grass. Naturally, the wrapped-up hot dogs land in the grass, and the naked watermelon slices get caked in dirt. I hate when that kind of thing happens.

    A very distinct noise cuts through the stillness of the woods, and a huge smile forms on my face. Rebecca is home.

    I crane my neck this way and that way but don't see her. It's not until I turn around that I spot my friend in the distance poking her head out from behind a fallen log.

    "C'mon girl," I coo. Even after all these years and having not shown much understanding of English, it's almost like she knows to come forward when I call her. I kneel down on one knee and spread my arms in greeting as she trots toward me.

    She's not aged well since the last time we were together. Gosh, how long ago was that? Four months?

    I laugh when I realize that the white fur around her nose has gotten even whiter. Rebecca tilts her head at me and those grey whiskers are going wild. Another breeze rips through the trees and her ringed, bushy tail flaps in tune with the wind.

    Rebecca must've noticed the food beside us because she looks at it, back at me, and back to the food. Little does she know, I've brought her favorite treat – orange dreamsicles. I take a step toward the watermelon and scoop it up before she can get her hands on it.

Rebecca makes a noise and I cock my head. Unfortunately, I still haven't caught on to even the basics of Raccoonese.

"C'mon, c'mon girl, follow me." As I lead her toward my picnic spot, I glance back every so often to see if she is still in tow. Eventually, we break through the trees and to the clearing where we always hang out.

The crescent moon hangs low in the starry night sky and all is still. I make eye contact with Rebecca and make a hand motion with the watermelon. She stretches out her short arms to grab it and I laugh as she desperately searches for water to clean the dirt off. Rebecca whips her head around to stare me down as if she's not amused. I reach in the basket for a Coke and drip a little over the watermelon. Rebecca retreats with her watermelon and chomps away.

Things are almost like they used to be.

I check my watch. It's late; I would think fireworks would've gone off by now. I spread out my blanket, lie down, and can't help but smile as the grass tickles my legs. Rebecca lets out a string of noises and comes to join me. She's pleased.

The first of many fireworks light up the sky as I reach into the basket for three dreamsicles – one for me, and two for Rebecca.

Time passes way too quickly as we enjoy each other's company and our treats. I really wish things could go back to the way they used to be.

It's not until the firework displays die down that Rebecca sprawls out on the blanket and falls asleep.

My arm reaches for the phone in my back pocket without second thought. I flip it over and find what I'm searching for in the back of the card holder.

The polaroid picture finds itself before my eyes without permission. There we were – the cutest couple on campus. It was the way he would hold my hand in public and tuck the loose strand of hair back behind my ear. A single tear wells up in my eye but for the first time, I refuse to let it fall out.

Inexplicably, Rebecca snuggles her head against my thigh. I glance down and find her black eyes locked with mine and I swear that there's a look of satisfaction dancing around in them.

A sudden gust of wind rips the picture out of my fingers and it all too quickly vanishes into the night sky. Rebecca purrs. I can't help but smile and this fleeting feeling of wanting to speak her language passes through me.

    Things are going to be okay for now.

By the White Boy Summer Grill
Inferno Corps

Profoundly sunny skies surround my home
As Chad and Larry grill the juicy steaks.
The feeling of a summer neon chrome,
Begins to lift my spirit, heals the aches.

Rhodesian green and crosses worn by all,
The boiz begin to pray for the great food.
The party starts, the drinks go 'round, we ball!
We dance to synthwave songs which set the mood.

Though Luke could not attend this awesome feast,
We know that he is happy up above.
The smell of ice cold beer and yummy yeast,
Now fills the air, as we recite our love:

A love for country and for our own kin,
We cheer for White Boy Summer once ag'in.

Untitled
Public Mogger

Peregrine found no solace in shadow. He lay by the body of water as he always had. A strange-looking leaf, blown by eastern wind went past him, not unnoticed. He lay one man's feet from it, yet did not paw at it, strength saved for a fight. The fox might come by tonight and he will protecc. There are chickens here.

He curled and uncurled himself. Smells, unfathomably many smells nearby. He recognizes almost all, starts a walk to greet master and find source of new smells. Greeted with touch where he grants it.

The settlement a dozen houses large, at night his domain. Rat killer. Ship keeper. The pier stretches long, small ships on one side, two large on the other. He was acquainted with the ships but every time they brought new smells and new vermin to be rooted out.

They stunk and he was hungry. A snack and a kill, in that order. Two at least, it made him look forward to when the large ships came back. If one escaped, the hunt was on. He would make a play of it. Leave the play pieces by master's door. Cat's honor.

Tampico
J.H. Meixner

Didn't you hear?

About what?

Old fool got waylaid up in a bed at Shannon. Had an accident in his garage. That goddamn truck he's always tinkering on came down on him. Mangled his foot something fierce – I knew he'd get bit by it sooner or later.

Never did feel comfortable when he was working. Once, Vic and I brought 'round my old Ranger - said he'd put new breaks if I brought 'em. Only wanted forty bucks and a case of Shiner for it. Couldn't find his chocks so he just put a stack of phonebooks behind the wheels. That jack of his was rustier'n shit too. Wouldn't ever get one to replace it. Can't help but feel sorry for folks who're sentimental about something like that.

The jack's what gave out after all. Seems he'd been pinned there for hell if anyone knows how long. Didn't have no phone nearby, couldn't call nobody.

Wouldn't've called nobody. Thompson doesn't have a phone at all. Arrogant fool. Always been one.

You got him all wrong, Moody. Just keeps to himself is all. He ain't much for troubling anyone.

Well he's got folks troubled now. Arrogant fool.

Hannah found him there. She's the one who drove him out to Shannon. Said she'd expected something like that to happen. Said after all that she figured something must've happened what with there being no wind. Not even cicadas chirping. Sweltering day like today with the seeds of thunderheads creeping up slow over the bluffs, not moving so much as a speck when you look no matter how long you look at 'em. An omen, she's always told me. Anyhow she's there with him so I reckon it'll all come out in a wash anyhow.

They had sat in silence for quite some time. It was strange that the cicadas had gone mum. The waters in the Concho appeared to him so placid as to start flowing back upstream. After the conversation had died Moody said his goodbyes and went back to Eden. The dancehalls in town these days only had old men around anyhow, he'd said. Too hot for any of the girls to come out. How they used to work up a real sweat, all the students pressing into each other, the men trying to pry the groups of women apart to have for themselves with all the deftness of cracking open freshwater mussels. Bodies stuck in an amalgam. Less a dance and more like passing flypaper through a swarm. He realized abruptly that Victor and Aaron had also fled but he couldn't pin down exactly when. Likely they had had enough of his problems and rummaged through their phones for any coed they could find to give them benign problems of their own. Idle leisure was a luxury that everyone else but him seemed able to afford.

    His guilt caught him once he was alone by the river. Too much stagnation. You and your pusillanimous ass. It makes me ill. You wouldn't let yourself get dragged out dancing with Moody no matter how much you'd even want to. Can't even go enjoy yourself without some excuse about why you aren't allowed to. To hell with the old man. You don't owe him a minute. Hannah will take care of Thompson. Just like she used to take care of you. A small breath moved his hair into his eyes. His feet scrambled for grip on the amber bottles he'd jettisoned and he retched as he tried to stand and his legs wobbled as if chains on a carnival swing. The windmills on the bluff radiated and wavered in the haze and fulgurous blooms flashed behind them in the roiling thunderheads and his chest resonated with each silent blast. To hell with the girls. To hell with Moody too. One or two of those dancehall geezers will still manage to conjure up some pale shade to dance with just because they decided it was worth it for them to be there, and you'll have just gone emptyhanded back to Eden. Coward.

    He finally got up on his feet but was still far from firm Earth and his head swam round and he wheeled and skated up the hill away from the fetid river, stumbling and stinking drunk, fishing blind in his pockets, first his shirt, then his pants and then his shirt again before he found his keys. The car stood silent vigil as he approached and he groped for the door handle and missed, retched, reached again and the handle slipped from the ocean of sweat in his hands, tried weakly yet again and felt a jolt of static as he finally made contact, heaving it open and losing his balance again from the force of it before slinking down inside. The heat even in the sinking sun was still oppressive and he hadn't the strength to close the door or even start the car. He didn't feel he'd deserve the relief that he'd get from the AC. It was just an artifice of relief anyhow. He slouched there, dumb for donkey's years. The silence was unbearable. He wanted to call Hannah, to use the old man as an excuse but his fingers were obstinate when he tried to command them and his gut sneered in mutiny and he cursed himself for having the temerity to even harbor such a desire. The sun hid away entirely behind the bluff and in the saturnine darkness out in the desert the thunderheads sparked silent admonitions to him as they watched over the town and he sank lower still into the car seat. He longed for the cicadas to speak.

Tarmac and Dreams
Arthur Powell

1.

The road opened up ahead. The heat shimmering off the worn asphalt. He opened the throttle kicking up a gear and adjusted his tucked position on the bike. It roared. A beast unchained. The road curved to the right and he gently began to push right on the handlebars easing the bike into the turn. His heart pounded as the corner continued to tighten.

Push right

Push right

He increased his pressure on the handlebars turning the bike further into the curve. Like a ballet dancer poised on stage the bikes tired rolled and gripped the road.

He saw the curve ending and began straightening the bike back up, gently opening the throttle further to accelerate out of the turn.

Glorious.

2.

"Refill for ya hun?"

He looked up at the aged waitress proffering the coffee pot.

"Sure." He smiled at her.

"My eldest was a biker" She sniffed "You aren't in a gang now are you?"

The concern was etched on her face, disappearing as he shook his head.

"No ma,am - just a lone wolf".

"Well ride safe, that'll be 15.90 at the counter when you're done."

He sipped his coffee and looked out the cafe window. It was nine am and the summer sun already bright and strong. Plenty of time for more riding. Maybe he'd cut down to the coast road before it got too crazy with traffic.

Life was simple on the bike. There was no passivity. Everything was deliberate, always. He drove a car like everyone else, was on his phone in traffic like everyone else. Not on a bike. No music, just earplugs. No distractions. Pure concentration. Death lurked everywhere, from the distracted soccer mom in their SUV to the raging boomer in their RV. Cagers are ragers.

3.

The coast road was always beautiful. The Pacific a glittering jewel. The traffic was picking up and the high-speed moments fewer and farther between. He cruised like all good bikers, enjoying the scenery. Other bikers flashing the universal 2 finger salute out enjoying the day.

It was as he came up on a traffic light he encountered them. The car accelerated turning in front of him, his quick reaction braking saving them for collisions.

"Fucking idiot" he swore under his helmet and blasted his horn, an anemic almost comedic toot like almost all bikes used. The aging yellow Subaru Baja's driver had clearly not seen him. Suddenly his blood was up and he accelerated to pull level with the car at the lights. He flipped his helmet up and lifted the sun visor and saw her.

She was not the driver but the passenger. Simply the most beautiful girl he'd ever seen. She smiled at him. Her blue eyes and freckles alive with energy. He was speechless. The driver suddenly leaned across and yelled.

"Sorrrrryyyy" before giggling. She then half flashed her tits as the beauty swatted at her friend's silliness still smiling at him.

The blast of a horn snapped him from his stupor. The cars behind were honking furiously and he looked up to see the Yellow Baja turning left away from him. He cursed and fumbled his bike into gear. But now the traffic was flowing and the turn signal red. His beauty was getting away. He revved the engine furiously waiting for the light to turn. He felt the sweat drip down in his helmet as the seconds ticked away. Finally the light changed and he took off after the Baja.

4.

It was gone. He couldn't find it. Dejected, he cruised the streets scanning left and right hoping it would be there but there was no sign of the Yellow Baja and the beauty who rode shotgun. He pulled over, stopped the bike, and looked out to the ocean. Somehow dusk had surprised him. The lengthening shadows and gentle waves slowly ushering in the night.

He trudged down to the shore barefoot and stood in the shallows. All felt lost. The water lapped at his feet as he gazed out. Darkness descended and he turned back to his bike.

Wait

There it was.

The Yellow Baja, he was sure of it. Parked right behind his bike. He scrambled to get his shoes back on and stepped out into the street. Empty. He scanned the street and saw the bar. They must be in there he thought.

5.

He slicked his hair back as best he could and walked in. Something about the armor padding of his motorcycle jacket gave him that confidence. That slight swagger in his step. The bar was lively but not yet full. With some purpose he strode to the bar looking for her, eyes glancing around.

He squinted, that there was the driver. Sat at a table with a guy animatedly telling some kind of story. So where was she?

"What you want to drink motoboy?"

Somehow he knew but didn't know all at the same time. A sense. There she was, his beauty coyly smiling at him from behind the bar.

He smiled.

"Shot of whisky and a Coors Banquet"

"Coming right up."

He felt on cloud nine. His heart pounded. The road suddenly opened up before him.

She deposited the shot and beer before him watching cooly as he knocked back the shot.

He raised the can to his lips, that first sip to chase the whisky.

"So, fancy a ride?"

She smiled.

Firefly Dance
Outgoing Misanthrope

Spring proceeds along apace
Humbly making her way towards an exit
As the thunderous Summer approaches
With all the crass bombast he brings

The seeds sprout after their slumber
As runners and shoots dash madly along
Staccato dance of root and branch
Like Winter was never a thing at all

The Moon shines down with serene aplomb
A quiet counterpoint in the Season of Sun
As the chitinous orchestra of rape-happy creatures
Weave the somnolent sonata that cushions the nocht

A study in dark;
Mute green-now-gray on midnight black.
But a spray of bright quickens the night
As the fireflies dance their way toward Dawn

Wouldn't it be Nice
Outgoing Misanthrope

    The dry heat felt good on his skin as he stared out over the sapphire blue water of what had to be the most perfect weather conditions he could imagine. Left to right, in long lingering gazes, he saw Earth and Sky meet at some unknowable point in a bright future. He could smell the suntan lotion and healthy bodies, their garish colored bathing suits standing out from an incredible distance. Sitting on the dunes, dashing around makeshift volleyball courts, wandering in that semi-solid place between the waves and the sand, and cavorting in the bathwater warm shallows; everyone he saw seemed synchronized. Looking down, his feet were slowly sinking into the water-laden sand with each onrush of seafoam, taking him down a few more millimeters each time. The grin that split his face was wide and welcoming, just like the powerful sun hanging in a sky with perfectly aligned clouds.

    Jim took off the headset and all of the effects aided by the pills and inputs disappeared in an instant. He made sure to save to hard disk and took a drink of potassium salt fluid to relieve his cottonmouth. Outside, the dingy sleet competed with the endless traffic noises for domination of the small porthole to a grim and gray world. The computer prompted him to name the new save file. He stared at the blinking cursor, thinking back to the carefree happiness that his brain was sure was his only moments ago, then tapped onto the touch screen: E N D L E S S _ S U M M E R

Heat of Formation
Outgoing Misanthrope

    The heat was competing with the humidity for control of the small talk as the last few screws were sunk. The combination of the two Hellion Sons of Summer made the timbers flex and curve just so, causing the man to question his double-measured cuts. Sweat was pouring off by the bucketful, and the soulless bugs of the high season were approaching their crescendo before the staggered exit to make way for the serenade of eventide crickets. The last glass of lemonade was bone dry, and the buxom angel wasn't going to wade through the sultry air yet again just to watch many minutes of loving stirs disappear down a parched gullet. The children had fled to the cold embrace of modernity, and even the loquacious neighbor had decided, for once, that discretion was the better part neighborliness, quitting his fence post vigil to lounge at the altar of the Almighty Flat Acreen, awash in the cool, artificial air for which all paid dearly.

    The drill was almost dead, and cleanup would be at least another 45 minutes, coinciding with that beautiful moment where the sky is bright as day but the sun has sunk just past the tree tops, so he submitted to the seductive breeze that had just kicked up from yonder. Stashing the screw gun and ditching the belt, he kicked off his boots, which dragged the sodden socks right along behind them. He wondered for the umpteenth time if there was any truth to the internet idea of "grounding," and whether or not it even mattered as the baked grass fronds bent and crackled beneath his toes and soles. The sun was punching through in a stunning inverse cucoloris, granting the leaves a few moments of God quality rim lighting in between green illumination and shadow. The tree bugs were different than the creepie-crawlies of the grass, their song being more unpacked and morose, and the staccato interruption of a woodpecker added a wondrous syncopation, such that before he knew it, he was through the dell and into the deeps, with a darksome quiet descending in a dress rehearsal for twilight.

    Here he stopped, and here he stood, the work of the day behind him and the revelry of summer nights with family just out of mind around the bend. He withdrew the makings and rolled a tobacco cigarette, his tobacco from his dirt, and sparked the moral joint with a deep inhalation that sent the caustic smoke to the tiniest corners of his lungs. He held onto it for a second past wise, then let it out, slow and steady, adding texture to the diminishing rays that managed to invade the canopy at just the right angle. He could feel the moment slipping, but he didn't cling to it. He had needed a respite from his self-imposed rigor, a simple moment to enjoy the things he fought to have for just a little while before age and urges traded places, and just as he had presumed, just as it always was...

The summer's moment was enough.

Independence Day
Aldo Jonsson

    I pulled up to Corey's house a little after two. Parking behind Ryan's Escort wagon and Derek's CR-X, I unstuck my legs from the vinyl seats of my brown '81 Corolla and stepped out onto the street. Tall fir and cottonwood trees shaded the whole cul-de-sac. I opened my trunk and removed my weapons: a sawed-off wiffleball bat and a shoebox full of bottle rockets. I walked around to Corey's backyard. I was the last to arrive. Ryan and Derek were taking turns doing flips on the trampoline. Big Dave, Little Dave, and Jordan were sitting in lawn chairs.

    "Hey!" said Big Dave, when he saw me coming around the side of the house. "Let's do this!"

    Corey came out of the house through the open sliding door, as Ryan and Derek jumped down to the thick, soft grass. Everyone grabbed their gear, much of it purchased on the rez that morning, and walked down the short hill to the vacant lot next door.

    There were to be no teams today. It was a battle royale. There would be no winners either. We'd go until someone got hurt, we ran out of steam, or out of ammunition. We all spread out, and Corey was first to fire, a devious grin on his face. He liked to fire straight from his garden-gloved hand. His shot was aimed at Jordan, but it was nowhere close.

    We ran around shouting and firing for the next ten minutes. Flick, hiss, whistle, pop. We laughed with every close call. A well-aimed shot from Ryan, guided by a length of PVC, hit me in the calf. It glanced off and exploded in the weeds a few feet away. I hit Derek in the back while he was lighting his next shot. Smoke billowed out from the end of my bat.

    The battle fizzled out spontaneously. Big Dave sat down, out of breath and with streams of sweat on his face. A couple of us were out of rockets. Little Dave showed off a cut on his neck where he had been grazed.

    Corey ran back to the house and returned with a special treat: an M-1000, said to have the explosive power of a quarter stick of dynamite.

    After some brainstorming, we decided to use it on a rusty 55-gallon drum in the middle of the lot. Ryan tipped the barrel onto its open side, leaving enough of a gap for the over-stuffed firecracker. Corey lit the fuse and tossed it under the barrel. We ran for it. We made it up to Corey's yard in time to turn and witness the explosion. The top of the drum, weakened by years of corrosion, launched high into the sky to the accompaniment of a resounding **BOOOOMMM** that shook the windows of the house. We watched the distant lid grow larger as it tumbled back to earth a few seconds later.

We were speechless. We were screwed. Half the town would have noticed that.

Jordan had the bright idea to get on the trampoline. The rest of us gathered around, acting casual.

Not two minutes later, a police officer came around the side of the house. His radio crackled as he approached. My stomach lurched.

"We got a call about some kids lighting off some bottle rockets. You guys wouldn't know anything about that, would you?"

My mouth clamped shut. No one moved. Ryan spoke up.

"No, sir. We're just jumping on the trampoline."

The officer gave us the look of a man just trying to tick boxes on a form. With his boot he nudged an open shoebox that was sticking out from under a lawn chair.

"Well, then make sure *your* bottle rockets stay put away. Have a good Fourth."

He left. We went inside.

Bonfire of the Inanities
Buff Chadwick

Fifteen years in prison for election interference. Reynard Brine was not numb. He had spent a month in jail since the sentencing and the creeping horror had grown more and more intense. If anything, he was hyper-alert. Every detail of his confined little world stood out like a gleaming crystal while the events of the past few years played endlessly on repeat in his head.

To those politically aligned, the hypocrisy was the worst part of the affair. Reynard had done nothing but post a meme encouraging the opposition to 'vote' by text message. If that were interference, he was far from the only man to have done it but those supporting the other candidate had not been prosecuted. For all that, it was not the hypocrisy eating up Reynard but the cruelty of watching his life stolen from out of his hands. Fifteen years!

The custody transport vehicle whizzed down the highway. The marshals had restrained him, though his charges were not of a violent nature. The windows in the prisoner compartment were tinted and opaque. He was alone. There was nothing to do but stew in his own dread.

The vehicle came to a stop. A minute later, two black marshals cracked open the back door to the van. One of them released his restraints and he stepped out of the vehicle. It was parked behind an abandoned gas station on the side of the tumbleweed-strewn highway, out of sight of the vehicles that roared past. One of the marshals freed Reynard from his handcuffs and he barely bottled up his panic. This was not prison and this stop was definitely not scheduled. Were they going to shoot him and claim he had been trying to escape? He stood frozen in place. The marshals yawned, slammed the doors on the van and drove off.

A 1972 De Tomaso Pantera pulled up. The driver looked like Steve McQueen. He pulled a cigarette out of his mouth.

"Need a ride, stranger?" He pulled down his sunglasses and winked with his startlingly blue eye. "Say, I don't know about that orange getup. People might mistake you for a convict. I got some spare clothes in the trunk. Try 'em on."

In a few minutes, they were speeding across the alkali desert with The Blue Danube resounding gloriously from a set of speakers rigged onto the Pantera's dashboard. The man who looked like Steve McQueen passed Reynard a Venezuelan passport. He was not too surprised to find his likeness staring back at him from the pages.

"You want me to go to Venezuela?" He asked.

"Nah," said the driver. "You're a 'fugee from Venezuela. Stay here! Don't worry about the prison. We did a little bribery. Some surveillance footage got lost. On the record, Reynard Brine is still behind bars. In a couple months, he'll suffer a heart attack. Vaxxed probably. He'll get cremated and that'll be the end of him."

Reynard laughed. "Who are you?"

"Hey, you can't go accidentally spilling secrets when you don't know them." McQueen smiled. "I'm just a friend."

Reynard laughed and laughed and laughed again. He could not hold it in. He had fantasized, of course, about an appeal, a pardon or even a Shawshank escape. Yet he had not even dreamed of this. His heart was fluttering like some little bird in spring. For this to be possible, the criminal system had to be massively corrupt but, then again, that it had convicted him in the first place was proof of that. There were too many people involved in his escape. It had to be sloppy but as long as no one had cause to investigate, the case of Reynard Brine would be swallowed up in the penitentiary swamp and be forgotten.

Sometime later, they pulled into Reno and parked at a suburban house built in the 60s. McQueen tossed him a set of keys.

"Welcome home, cowboy."

"You bought this for me?"

"Ha! No way. The taxpayer bought it for you. Somebody has to pay for the refugees. You'll get regular financial assistance and there's talk they're going to open up social security for you guys too. Oh hey, I almost forgot. Don't get fingerprinted again. We couldn't get to that database."

The house was a little cramped and creaky, with decades of slow decay, but it was pleasant and not a cell. There was even a pool in the yard with flamingo floaties bobbing around. A handful of people cheered and greeted Reynard by the name on his Venezuelan passport. They all acted like he was an old friend and they kept asking how he had escaped from the commies. There was pizza and balloons and those simple things suddenly made him as happy as they had felt when he was a kid.

When the party wound down, Reynard caught McQueen just as he was stepping into the Pantera.

"Hey, I just…" Barely, Reynard succeeded in holding back his sudden tears. "Thank you so much for… for all of this. I was anon. VPN and everything. The feds wouldn't even have known who I was if some pondslime in the group chat hadn't ratted me out. All this time, you know, all through the trial, I've been stewing over him but I guess a good friend more than makes up for a traitor."

"Hey," McQueen shrugged. "They were funny memes."

He roared off down the road and the Pantera dwindled into the Sierra Nevadas.

We Are So Back
Anthony Stryker

    I wasn't ever much of a golfer but here I was, stuck in these silly clothes, toting around a bunch of clubs I don't really have any idea what to do with. At least God blessed us with a cool breeze and slight overcast. The birds were singing and I couldn't help but think how nice it would be to wet some fishing lines in that lake we just passed. Just as my childhood friend Mike went to tee off, I was thinking, "how'd he sucker me into this?" as we heard a slight thud, seemingly in the distance, and everything went oddly quiet. The chirping birds, no more. No car engines whining, brakes screeching. Nothing. Not a sound. We looked at each other in confusion as suddenly the clouds opened up and as the sun raced through and breathed warmth on our cheeks, a great spirit, what I would liken to an angel, appeared in front of us. There was no fear. A great peace came over as a giant man lays his hands on our shoulders, bagpipes start to play and a Scottish voice echoes through the hills, "go forth, brethren, WBS is upon us, no, I will not elaborate" and just as fast as the great spirit appeared, it was gone, but Mike and I both knew what had to be done.

    Commence White boy summer

Adolescent Longing
HNK

Your days are spent laid up at the public pool, spending what few dollars you have on popcorn and Powerade.

You go for an occasional dip in the pool to cool off but you aren't keen on swimming for long. When you grow bored you take a short walk over to the ice cream parlour where you have what could be called a romantic encounter with the *girl next door,* Becky—who, after this summer, you will never see again. But don't worry, there will be plenty of Becky's in your future.

You go home after having a few laughs and spend the night reading a book you're halfway vested in. *I Had A Hammer, The Hank Aaron Story.* You aren't an avid reader but you like baseball, and you liked Hank Aaron so you make an effort to read it.

Before going to sleep you yearn for the ocean, so in the morning, a little after dawn, you catch a bus to the pier. It's early and the city is quiet. You revel in the thought of being a ghost, and float through the sand listening to the calming swell of the sea.

Hours pass and people start to come out in droves. Around noon you goad on a man standing by the convenience store to buy you a tall beer, giving him a few dollars and telling him to keep the change.

Yeah why not, you look like it ain't your first time he said. Which is true, because Mike has a fake.

You have no idea what day it is or what day it was yesterday or what day it will be tomorrow and you don't particularly care. This is exactly how you like it. Finish your beer and lay on the sun soaked sand even though it's near too hot for bare skin. End up falling asleep for however long and wake up slightly sun burnt. No big deal. There's a bottle of Aloe Vera at home.

Leave the beach and grab a hot dog and coke from one of the guys beside the pier and eat it while walking down the sidewalk.

Check the time with someone who's selling shaved ice—3:21pm. Probably getting time to head home soon.

There's more lounging to do elsewhere.

Around five you catch the bus back home and wander the streets of your neighborhood for a while.

The background noise is vibrant and plentiful, kids are laughing, a sprinkler on a loop is watering the lawn, plistering back and forth, and the feint hum of cicadas can be heard as the sun begs to make its descent. Charcoal and sweat are prominent in the air as the sun turns a golden orange.

You'll do much of the same tomorrow. You're 17 this Summer, and you always will be.

Sweltering on I-35
Jorge G

    My groan rumbles under the grinding of the dying engine. Scalding steam rises into the night air as we pull over to the I-35 concrete barrier. We walk over the day's cracks in the asphalt and lean over the barrier. The cars 20 feet below spin as vertigo creeps over me. Your arm around my shoulder stabilizes me.

    "Relax." You say as I close my eyes and tug me in.

"Just hate looking like I stood her up." I say back as the 90 degree night air makes our sweat drip. A hot bead trails along your reassuring smile.

    "There's always next semester, other girls." You say as you watch the car headlights crawl along down below.

    "...whatever..." I mutter into my palms and you wipe your brow with your t-shirt. The glint of your skin in the full moon light gimmers in my tired eyes. "Night's fucked."

    Your hand, wrapped in your shirt, rubs over my warm forehead, then down along my flushed cheeks, and along my tight neck muscles. "Still time to pick something up, my place is close." You say as you turn over with your bare back against the barrier. Your lithe body outlines in the tow truck's headlights as it arrives.

    "...Sure. Thanks." I respond after gulping down the lump in my throat. The sound of the tow truck hauling my car up masks my gasp as you take your hand in mind without asking. Our sneakers kick up bits of gravel as you tug us over to the passenger side of the tow truck. We get in, our fingers entwine, and I think I should try something different next semester, starting tonight with you

Uncoveted
T.B.C.

    Seneschal seachord - the sound, the pier, the luger-cackles seamless, seen-mess messi-dorian soccer-wilson nearad rokkit-bowl richochet semi-scorianes haematidin' volleybawls, burr'd beer-shotguns, the summertime veranda of splotchean virescence her glutes trap-a-zhoi'd - done-ons exorbitant yewth hypnotizm through grewth'd, through mondegreens against the future-greening of ageasian greenhoused complacenceree. she sees u and u c hurr and understanding absolves solvency blur - her's padfooted, aboulia-mooted, sipping spirit redcap't like a naiad in dàyàn-equilabiam - bedlam and lambed-bedding a giver's givane - urs, excusing the re-fused-ree-fusal use of a griffith-behelit, the strangest coral-conch - castles my hand - put a there's yours-astared, ma'am-asita - spark of asterism when the cuticles connect - stands your martial bannerman up, creance a band-hawk's fianchetto'd godevermoired. the irreverence of hao u act tactfully sutures auwp a rift - all too's-well spurned - unoccoarred.

    Her converse - bayadereignin' the night awaie, glowkicks sketch-an-etchoplasmatic blessing heirosoal threwaot der venue ov God's endless cerulean amphitheatre. y tf dew these exorbitantlee compensated, sated-pen-mockean cunts viscera-gwata flaunt the value their eweveiling onlee - dsn't- valorize eetcelph bie 2daie? -a you- wondahrs, exterminatoring verso-recto set-so ov tracable ocean cradle-rockbacks peripherized - but then there isn't a thang but'd the eternal she out thurr awn lawnghawser'd lighttime díonyssum time vro, out sayonara na-ragiri, häkä-gure harakiri harkenin the hauberk'd kirinponche-poncho ov a night oint-solecismoe'd surfboard stellargenteily - flights 2 foam, strifes unstriven splasherations, mighty pearly whites given tongue-tied waie 2 spewing up ur thrush of surf lobbed @ her, laughtar limning a tailing orison tinctured-ohre - the great much less more than the less-mored gushless, grating gumption ov awl those denied b4 u dove to her herr-soul-rescue - to recuse their refusal ov fussillade'd sillage, to refuse the refuseless kissing finish - wat elewds eets image, wat denudes freighted diminishish, frightfoal, diligent, stowed 4 nao behind sinkean sunbeam plow. the new, true extirpatience within her smoulder-simony-gavage-gaze, hammock-quiver rin-tin-tin din quimescent.

no converse on the sand outside spumerasure. no converse in cliffside peregrine-dive, all rictus and no limits of god asymptotinge-cleavin' seicherished water-ply. no converse to sprezzatura - to maruta, to kickstand-quickhandialien-karuta 'wazu-neeee-eee, to daruta's rutting, la ruta's sputter, to splashing with sudden flings scattering awl accards starblazean beneath pointilist pinpriaptics awarded askar - to sudden reach reiching rench-ream - to poise impeached, peach-garden oath thanatophobia thrown away to pursue monstrance'd new-death creatine - for "crete", reading "conk-retic" - to nothing in its own deceit. i crete cons and you create preponderance precipitatives persipitation per's pic-a-city hoe will not poseidon and you, poseidon through her, i-don posse epsom salt ipso-facto sous videan a duo in 'pidermal-plastic duodendum MUGEN menstra strain nitrateless (and she knows nada baot nada baot habla lingua phrankalee wtf ur awn baot but acquiesces, slings her body to ur arms, initiates the first quine-lip of your ending infinite osculates absconding with into-the-night's), i'm-skateless auwf hao the heliacal takes us daon undertower'd riptide, strips bikini and slipslide-geta'd swim trunk and schleps us together, stipples forever brine-bettar'd, snips petit morts eanto mesquite pork-shoulder bone-ean slow roasts, rotisserie sitor-serial - the waters scilicettean a new-sprung season, one hundread poems d'over-cliffnoted in the stroke ordereds moating you and courtee-donin-whorus.

     Droplets stopping time off her depilative katabasis shoulder-drive, charibdyan churn in the cozy cove scouted to formulate the new-pass homecomean and your heart inside raises and praises and pleases and prays, hoalds awn, groans 4 her 2 stop and then opts itself to come to fruition, her legs wishbone-pullulari'd spread to ensure ur press connects her all-of self-evictive notice, the rite offeran 2 zeus' nous nothing more and nothing less converse than philiaharmonizean years-yièrs'd converse-yearn, your oyster confirmed in her pearling - nacre-cardinal accreting, lanid-drac's s'card-dinalide confiddo-secretarianarial, a hounding hoam-hõiminarete'd homilectic, resounding aegis-pitched, pounding hard-contrastid headin' upward as your's contractions-incumbents beachhead recumbencee:

     Keep us here forever. keep us clean, keep us preglass-corrugate, dune dunlin-drunken, keep us umkempt tempestuous-steradian, raiding new morns out mourn-forms, keep us spritzed on seafoam's lapping-abreast, keep us azimuthing to and from all deaths but the ones that parallel this twiddling in fingertips, laughline aligned tangency, her gaze gazelle-gazettean garlands to gallantry - keep us on the watch, soelsentinels sliding through the fonatelles of mollusk-looted mirepoix our gyri'd-wavelines blan-ketus. keep you here, gone's sweetest dearing, a gelid steed to steer, rhumblinearing lineate meering's subbuglio glide-on entourage encoring none, at longing's last-long long-lasted, against aghastless'd dancing, dancing, dancy deathless clearing - this fathering re-sonte.

From Another Satisfied Customer
CouchBod

Dear WBS Apparel®,

    I'm writing to you in order to express my gratitude for the way in which your fine products have changed my life.

    A little background. I am a 25 year old white male, skinny, never good with the ladies, no friends. I work a job as a junior law associate. I have been described by my superiors as "a good worker", "eager to please" and "shows up on time".

    I have my T-levels taken at my doctors, usually bimonthly. Previously, my numbers have been low and declining. However, since I have started wearing the WBS Apparel® Mogger 9000 tank top, my doctor has been seeing numbers of up to 9000 ng/dL. I would expect he would still be seeing such numbers. However, I received a call last week from his office informing me that his test equipment has been repeatedly malfunctioning every time he runs my fluids. He informs me he suspects the measurement is being overloaded!

    I try to keep myself in good shape at the gym and wearing WBS Apparel® reinforces my commitment to vitality and the fitness lifestyle. The other day, I was working out wearing my "Put it back" shirt while using the elliptical, my preferred machine. Some guy was using the squat rack and he just walked away when he was done, not re-racking the weights. Well, I think it was time to teach him a lesson. I swiftly moved between him and the door to the gym. One look at my shirt and he started tearing up and apologizing profusely, and this guy was at least 6'5", 250 lbs. This speaks to the profound message that the WBS Apparel® brand represents.

    This summer, thanks to WBS Apparel® products, I finally had the courage to venture up to my apartment building's rooftop pool. There are many pretty women up there, sunbathing and reading nonsense books. Not owning a swimsuit I donned only the WBS Apparel® GLOC sunglasses (in the Octavian Orange colorway), Axios Training Bag, and Squirreljack Fleece Beanie. As soon as stepped out into the pool area, one woman, previously sunbathing, immediately stood up, lowered her sunglasses and stared at me.

She was blonde, wearing a black ruched Vilebrequin® string bikini over a 4 class per week Pilates body. One glance at her haunches indicated that she was extra diligent with the bungee kicks. Above the waist, she was no Sydney Sweeney, being more on the aristocratic side, but nobody's perfect.

"Are those the WBS Apparel® official Glasses of Color (GLOCs) in Octavian Orange? I love WBS Apparel®. The men who work there are extremely masculine, handsome, and intelligent. True alpha chads. These qualities are also present in their customers. "

"These are indeed the WBS Apparel® Glasses of Color (GLOCs) in Octavian Orange. " I answered.

We locked eyes. Through the GLOCs she saw a future to believe in, a future that every single American would be excited to participate in.

As I spoke, I could see her front teeth bite down on her plump, red lower lip. Her eyes narrowed. Her cheeks flush, she breathed in sharply.

At that moment, I knew she was with my child. I left the pool area.

The next Monday, I showed up to work wearing three WBS Apparel® Axios Training bags over my Navy J. Press® suit. Underneath my dress shirt I wore a 1911 pattern WBS Apparel® "It's the Law in Kennesaw" ® t-shirt. The WBS Apparel® Axios Training bag is an essential part of my EDC. I wear one in front, one in back and the last is worn over the shoulder. In addition to my keys, knife, and two handguns, (Wilson Combat Commander 1911 and Colt Anaconda revolver), I fill any additional bag space, of which there is much, with WBS Apparel® Throw Away shades. Not only are these useful when sunglasses are needed, but they can also be used as a projectile weapon should I run out of ammunition.

Anyways, I get called into my bosses office. She is a brunette, in her forties, wearing plastic rimmed cat-eye glasses. This time, I notice she's wearing perfume. Her lips are red from lipstick. Her blouse seems one size too small today and for some reason the top three buttons are undone. For the first time I notice her bust, which was, if I dare say, Sweeneyesque. She walks in behind me, high heels clattering and closes the door. I move to sit down but she interjects.

"There's no need for that. "

She starts talking about how her husband is always busy and how lonely she's feeling. She moves closer, leaning in.

"I really like those training bags."

She reaches out her manicured hands and her fingers grasp my Anaconda through the Training bag.

"Ohh what's this?" she purrs.

The WBS Apparel® Throw Away shades rattle around.

"It's the law in Kennesaw." I respond.

I was intoxicated by the perfume and the smell of her breath.

Then I remembered I was going to be a father. I reached into my rear training bag and pulled out one pair Throw Away shades and smacked her across the face. She let out a shriek of rage and confusion. I threw Throw Away shades at her as I moved towards the office door to make my escape.

When I got home, I collected Ms. Vilebrequin, put my life and laundry in a Gladstone® bag, got in my red 2006 BMW® Z4M and headed south. She did not object to interruption of her scheduled Pilates classes. This speaks to the prestige and influence of the WBS Apparel® brand. During the drive we had a long discussion about how Julius Caesar did nothing wrong.

Unfortunately, I can't go into more details of the aftermath due to legal issues, but let's just say I am enjoying my White Boy Summer eating the fruits of a very lucrative sexual harassment lawsuit.

Thank you WBS Apparel®.

Chadwick Snodgrass, Esq.
Acapulco, Mexico, June 11, 2024

Supply Run
Graiser Blondifo

A blast of cold air welcomed him into the store. Frank and the boys had a few hours of daylight before the ring of fire at the lake, and he was tapped for provision acquisition.

He flashed a smile at the cashier. Her freckled cheeks lifted briefly in response. She brushed a few stray red strands behind her ear before her thin inkless wrists resumed restocking the buns by the roller display.

An entire world bloomed within her eyes. He could imagine her dangling her legs off the dock. She wouldn't be too scared to board the boat. She'd play along with the banter between his friends. He could see sunlight reflecting off the water onto her tanned legs, smell the scent of the bonfire as she curled up close to him.

There was a family standing by the beef jerky. Some kind of Mexican. One of them was a retarded boy. He stared blankly at the display of American flags, hats, and sunglasses. Frank grabbed a 30 rack from the walk-in. He stepped past a fat tourist woman and her scrawny male companion and grabbed two of the largest white energy drinks he could find.

"Y'all have a good day now" came the cashier's voice as she rang up another customer. It echoed within Frank's mind. He imagined its tone playfully thwarting his advances on a first date. He heard it rise in laughter, sharpen in acutely focused frustration with his antics, then glide down into whispers across his pillow.

Their coupling was a given. The years side by side on the steppes, shielding her from the wind, raising happy children, tending to wounds, carrying beauty through to old age- he saw it all clearly as he moved towards the register.

A hunched biomass covered in a faded windbreaker entered, the a/c blast swishing against his sleeves. Patches of his garb were made up of discarded shopping bags.

From the man's throat emanated fragments of conversation, phrases with no clear meaning or direction. No earpiece. He spoke to himself, or to anybody unfortunate enough to come within range.

Frank placed the beers and other items on the counter. The vagrant continued his ramblings, punctuated by collecting phlegm in scraping coughs.

Fear bubbled up in the cashier's eyes before looking up to Frank and smiling as she scanned his items.

"scuse me scuse me, y'all got a bathroom?" the man had swished his way towards the counter.

"It's for customers on-"

The homeless man lurched forward and snatched at the cashier's wrist, his bag covered hand raising up to aim a pistol at her. The cashier recoiled back, fumbling for the corded phone by the time clock.

Frank widened his stance and launched forward into him. Nothing could have prepared him for the smell. Months of ass sweat mixed with lemon. He pinned him to the ground with a knee on his back, his left arm hooked around his neck.

The Mexican boy stared, mouth agape, at the two men on the ground. The fat tourist moved her hands in a flurry, desperately trying to document the conflict. The soft boy muttered a "Hey man" before he was drowned out by the vagrant's screams.

The assailant's breath became rough, strained, as Frank's grip flexed. His incessant ramblings moved from human speech to animalistic gasps. "You picked the wrong place," Frank chuckled back to him. For a moment, the wretch's arms flailed upward in an attempt to get himself free. The heel of Frank's hand crunched his forearm downward, sending the hobo's pistol skittering across towards the door. Through a compressed windpipe, Frank could barely hear "dindu nuffin", then one pathetic final spasm and he released, leaving the attacker in a heap on the beige tile.

Frank stepped up, a small circle of dazed onlookers behind him. He collected his bag, adding "And I'll need 20 on pump 4, thank you".

The cashier stared at the scene, the cash sitting there on the counter.

Out by his truck, Frank slipped a pouch between his upper lip and gums and started the pump. Leaning one arm against the vehicle he surveyed the long stretch of highway in the valley below. No sirens, no lights approaching. A familiar voice sounded from the direction of the shop.

"Thanks for stopping that guy," the cashier shielded her eyes with a hand.

Frank nodded.

"I'm meeting some friends by the lake, would you be headed that way?"

"Sure am" Frank returned the nozzle to the pump. "I know a great spot to watch the fireworks."

I'm Dreaming of a White Christmas
Daniel McCloud

      Ah to be Mayor of a small town has so many perks. I can say to the chief of police " we don't have a issue with Germans here in fact we embrace them, let's replace the Shepherds with coon hounds"& the next day it happens. Or my favorite, todays festivities, CHRIST-MAS in July. There was a little push back when it was first brought to the table. " Can it be holly jolly in the heat"? To which I replied " this is south Texas weather is always the same Linda"! I 'll learn that dudes name one of these days, maybe around the time he learns if you're a dude with a earring & intern under me I am calling you a chicks name.

      As I walk to the stage I take the long way around the square to soak it all in. There's the classic car show, hot rods & big boats with bench seats fill this section. (After my speech, the prize for best father & son restoration project will be announced. I'm glad I'm not deciding that to many to choose from.) Next is big Pete's Texas bbq, the smell of brisket & burning mesquite is enough to drive you wild, the adding of the loud David Allan COE song is just marketing genius. I buy a cup of coffee & put a order for some chocolate chip cookies and milk from the lady who runs the best bakery in town who did a great job on her Mrs. Claus costume. Earnest saves Christmas will be playing at the drive in to end the day, got to have a treat while enjoy such a epic film.

      The roasted cowboy coffee goes down smooth, the heat doesn't bother me as much as not having it would, standing there looking at the little town who is looking to me to give a word to the Luke chapter 2 scripture I just read(felt a little funny dressed in cargo shorts, Santa fishing Hawaiian style shirt shades and a Santa cap to read such Holy words) "My friends I read these words to remind us regardless what season we are in Jesus Christ is the reason." " Although our town is a part of a nation that is falling apart let us be a example by keeping Christ in our hearts & putting up our shopping carts"!

      "Merry Christmas to all and to all a good night"!

The Serpent
Nathanael Hart

The old soldier stood fishing upon the beach. All about him, the heady joy of summertime was in full swing. Volleyball dudes and girls in bikinis, sandy bums and sandcastle builders; yet there he was, in full uniform, ankle-deep in the lapping waves, his eyes fixed with grim determination on the bobbing tackle.

His uniform was faded with time. His lapel bore a medal of honour, now tarnished by the long days of constant salt spray. At his hip was slung the sabre they had given to him as recognition for his long years of service. He had retired here, to the seaside town of his childhood, with a sizeable military pension and a plot of land to call his own. It should have been the perfect life. But he could not relax, could not relent, for he knew the *truth*.

Somewhere out there, in the glinting cerulean waters, twisted the Serpent.

A primordial beast of unfathomable devilry and wicked hunger. Its infinite coils waited, brooding, beneath the traitorous foam. If given the chance, it would rise from the water and devour him, his people, his home.

He wouldn't give it that chance. No; he would catch *it* first.

His country may have been finished with him, but he could not rest, not here, not in his home. The Serpent only needed him to slip up once. And so he cast his line again, salt lapping at his boots, and waited.

He heard splashes as something approached him from behind. Instinctively, he glanced – two young women in swimsuits, water glistening on their sun-touched skin.

"You've been out here all day, 'Captain'," cooed one of the girls. They'd come to speak with him before.

"Why don't you come have a drink with us," echoed the other, putting a soft hand on his shoulder.

"Can't," said the old man, "I'm fishing."

"We've got a cooler of beer. You must be so hot in that uniform…"

"You should get back to shore."

The girls put their arms around him. One lay her head against his arm, the other played with his officer's hat. He just stared out at the water.

"Don't tell us you're staying out all night again. It's going to storm later."

"Can't leave," growled the soldier, "Serpent's still out there."

The girls giggled. "Oh come on. He's never shown up. You've never even seen him."

"I don't need to see him. I know."

"Oh Captain my captain! Won't you just leave it? Come and have a drink with us."

"No."

They pouted. "Fine, suit yourself." And they paddled away.

In the distance he heard someone call to them. "Stop talking to that crazy asshole. You've got no idea what he's on."

They didn't get it. They couldn't get it. But that was fine, that was the way of things: he alone would bear this weight.

In the distance he could see the truth of their words. Black clouds, creeping over the edge of the world, full of anger and fury and hate.

Let them come, he thought. He drew back his line and cast it again.

###

The wind howled, the rain lashed, the air was dark with threat. But there upon a rocky outcrop stood the old soldier, stance wide to hold his ground, fishing rod held firmly in hand.

A great wave smashed against the rock, white foam cascading over his already soaked body. Lighting flashed in the distance, thunder cracked and bellowed its direful warning.

And then, amidst all the rage about him, he felt the line tug.

His body lit up like an electric fire. This was it, this was the moment. He pulled on the line – nothing, like pulling on a boulder. He summoned all of his strength and pulled again.

With a roar and an earth-shaking groan, something enormous rose from the water. Lightning glinted off its scales; water and seaweed dripped from its monstrous body; its mouth was crammed with fangs sharp like the doom of men; and at the top of it all were its eyes, white eyes, glaring at him with viscous intent. The Serpent, in all its terrible splendour.

He dropped the fishing rod and drew his sword. "Come on, you bastard," he spat, "let's finish this."

The Serpent opened its maw and lunged. The soldier reared his sword and leapt. The lightning cracked. And the thunder boomed.

###

The next morning, the sky was crystal clear again and the waters were as calm as ever. There was no sign that a storm had ever happened. The beachgoers began to filter onto the sand for another day of summer fun. But what they saw shocked them: no longer did the old soldier maintain his silent vigil; no longer did he stand there fishing.

Instead, he sat upon a fold-out chair before a fire of his own construction. Above the flames he held a metal poker, on which was skewered a massive chunk of scaled meat. Sprawled in the shallows behind him, taking up almost the entire length of the beach, was the body of an enormous serpent.

The two women stood before him, mouths agape. He held up the skewer. A good soldier knew that nothing should be wasted – but more than that, he knew the only way to celebrate victory was with a good meal.

He cleared his throat with a smile. "Care for breakfast?"

Float
Dillon Hamilton

"So, there I was trying to pick my nose like a normal person at the back of the Walmart parking lot when this wench, looking like an oil baron's wife, taps the glass of my window with the edge of a metal dog cage, saying, 'Help me! Help me!'" Austin started his story as the four of them shoved off the manmade rocky beach on the Illinois River.

From the bow of the canoe, Chandy thought the two months since graduation had done Austin more than a little good. The way he shoved the three of them from the shore and leaped into the back of the canoe without getting wet proved he had regained his preseason vigor that she had seen from the stands in the early Spring games. He wore a black tank top with the obscure lyrics of an early aughties punk song. His trunks were salmon and sure to be stained by food or mud by the end of the lazy float. A beer cracked open in the middle of the canoe, breaking Chandy's meditation on Austin.

"You better have found twenty dollars at the end of this story or I won't care," Casey said before guzzling down half a beer.

"You couldn't wait three seconds from shore before you cracked open a cold one?" Jordan asked.

"The worst part is that they aren't even cold, yet. Bought 'em at the gas station thirty minutes ago and Bino's dumbass forgot to put ice in the ice chests until just before we hopped in the boat," Casey complained.

Chandy finally had the chance to solve a mystery that had intrigued her for the past two years. "I've never understood why you all call him Bino."

"He has clear skin! Like an albino!" Jordan said. "Wasn't that obvious?"

As he paddled, Austin added, "Next time you see him look at his eyebrows. They're white."

Open season on Bino's appearance continued, but what Austin had said, *Next time you see him*, brought back a fear for Chandy. She had made real friends at Connors State College even though she had looked down on them all in the beginning. Now, she feared there may not be a next time to see Austin.

"How many canoes did our group rent?" Casey asked.

"Three and one raft," Austin said.

Casey started counting his fingers.

"That's somewhere between one hundred and twenty and one hundred and sixty beers," Austin said.

*

One mile downriver Casey and Jordan were tipsy enough to take off their shirts and brave the lukewarm mix of fluids, leaving Austin and Chandy behind in the canoe.

"That idiot nearly tipped us over," Chandy said, gesturing toward Casey.

"He's improving. He tipped us over on the Freshman float and thirty-three beers went with him," Austin said.

"He lost thirty-three beers?"

"Nope. Swam like a madman and recovered ever single can and stole three IPAs from a neighboring ship," Austin said.

Chandy giggled her way into a flushed face. "How have you been enjoying your summer? And why are you so tan already?"

"My cousin owns a directional boring company. We've been drilling polylines for fiberoptic cable out west. It's mostly on county roads. We might get one or two cars to pass us all day so I only wear shorts and rarely a hardhat."

"Isn't that dangerous?"

"Depends on who you ask."

"What are you plans after that?"

Austin tossed her a beer and opened one for himself. "I'm enrolled at OU. I don't have plans once I get there." He drank the entire can, smashed it, and placed it back in the ice chest next to a small stack of other crushed cans. Chandy realized he was counting.

*

When the float had ended, Austin and Chandy had broken away from the group to avoid Casey's drunken rant about how they all should have had a group photo near a particular outcropping along the river. They hopped in Austin's truck and drove back upriver a few miles to the gas station where they had bought their beer before the float. Austin told Chandy to leave her purse in the truck grab anything she wanted, but she insisted to pay for herself because she was hungry. She took a bag of jerky, a Pepsi, and a bag of peanuts to the counter. The man behind the register tallied her total and asked, "You with him?" pointing to Austin.

"Yes."

"Must have an ID. He buy beer."

Austin laid the twelve pack on the counter. "What!"

"She with you. You buy beer. I need both IDs. It's the law."

"No, enough of that nonsense. Let her pay and then I'll pay for *my* beer with *my* ID."

The man gave Austin a look that made Chandy uncomfortable.

"Fine, Mr. Talkie Talkie. Total is twelve seventy-two."

Chandy handed him a twenty. He began gathering her change, "You know we can get in a lot of trouble for not IDing her. Here your change, ma'am. We can lose the license for the beer. You wouldn't like that."

In a moment, Austin to a stick of beef jerky from its container in the counter and slapped the man across the wrist. "Count it out!"

"Hey! Watch it talkie bastard."

"I said count out the lady's change."

The man's hand slowly reached for the cash register where he took a five-dollar bill and added it to her change and handed it to her without counting it out. "Go to the truck, Chandy. It's unlocked," Austin said.

*

Austin sipped his beer and Chandy drank her Pepsi and peanuts, while they sat on his tailgate facing away from the group bonfire and staring at a small cliff face across the river.

"How did you know he shorted me?" Chandy asked

"They do that. They distract you and short your change or mess up a vendor's check on purpose. I've seen it too often. It's like a cultural virtue for them to deceive a white man," Austin almost murmured. "I hate it."

"Well, you won't see much of us after this. You'll be at OU and the rest of us will go our ways as well," Chandy said, masking the intense desperation she felt.

"I'll see you," Austin said.

"Already planning next year's float?"

Austin took her hand from the edge of the tailgate. "No, I'll see you."

Rockport Crusher
@Degreestudies

In June of 1997, Bobby lost his fear and began to love his grandfather. He was eight that summer, just turned, and like every summer before, he spent it in Rockport, Maine.

This time was different, though. Usually Bobby's family made a slow trip from their home in Providence up the coast. They would stop for a weekend of camping at Nickerson State Park on the Cape, and then pause in Boston for a Red Sox game and the Children's Museum. And usually Bobby looked forward to the first leg of the journey, but not the part at his grandparents' house --- where odd smells and odder behavior dominated his memories.

But this summer, Bobby was informed that they would head straight to Maine, doing the four-and-a-half hour drive in one go. Bobby's eyes had welled up with tears at the surprising news. His normally good-humored father had looked at Bobby like he wanted to yell, and his mother had leaned down close and whispered, "I know it's hard to understand, sweet-pea, but Pa Harry is sick. He just had surgery, so we want to spend more time with him and Grams."

For the whole drive, Bobby stared out the window or looked at his Roger Clemens rookie card while his twin sisters napped in car seats on either side of him. Bobby's father, who usually told stories or played I-Spy on the long ride, was staring silently ahead, and didn't even turn on the radio. The family arrived at Bobby's grandparents' house without the usual fanfare, just quiet hugs and more silence. Bobby's parents got to work almost immediately, cleaning up the house and waiting on Pa Harry. This really wasn't like other summers at all, Bobby thought. But after a few quiet, unhappy days, the tension finally broke.

That morning, Bobby's mother, Grams, and the twins had gone down to the beach while Bobby stayed behind, drawing in his coloring book on the wide welcoming porch. Pa Harry rocked nearby in his favorite chair while Bobby's father prepared hot dogs on a little green propane grill they always took camping. Whenever Bobby thought his grandfather was asleep, he'd steal quick looks at the man, noting his shabby denim overalls and the pipe that was always hanging in the corner of his mouth. Every few glances, Pa Harry would catch him in the act and would wink and smile at the boy. Bobby's eyes would quickly dart away.

It was after one of these cat-and-mouse games that Bobby noticed his father's smile.

Pa Harry laughed. "Ma grandson wants ta know why his fathah is smilin, doncha Bobby?" Bobby looked back and forth between the two men, confused now, but also relieved to see they were both grinning.

Bobby's father said, "Ok Dad, tell Bobby what you told me last night. Tell him why you weren't afraid to go under the knife."

Real laughs now, and then Pa Harry motioned Bobby to come closer, so the boy scooted his butt along the sandy porch to sit at his grandfather's feet.

"You knaw Ah'm a lobstah trappah, a bug trappah, I was anyway." Bobby's dad was really laughing now and Pa Harry went on, "Oh sorry son, a lob-ster trapp-er."

"Well I told ya fathah this last night. He thinks Ah'm full of shi- full of it. But you'll believe me. I trapped lobstahs for 40 years up heah in Maine, even had my own boat for a while. One time, I think this was in 1971, we're haulin owah traps, and Ah'm takin bugs out on tha deck, and I get ta one and I see that this bug has actually stove-up my trap with his claw. Shouldn't be possible for a bug ta do that, but two of tha wooden cross hatches were all stove ta hell. Sadly fo' this fellah, traps have wire inside tha wood, and this bug, it punctuhed his left crushah. I could tell that crushah was rooned. So I cut off his crushah and…

"You knawa bug, they can't really look at ya, you can't follaw a bug's eyes so much, but he tuhned his head ta me and I knew he wanted ta be free. I thought ta myself, well Ah've been trappin' a few years and Ah've nevah seen a bug stove da trap so if this bug's tryna tell me he wants ta be free he's said it pretty cleah, ayuh. So I look around and all tha otha' fellas are busy with their wohk so I toss this bug back ovah tha side.

"That first time I nevah told anyone. I was shy about it. I had a reputation for bein' soft on animals, soft in the head your Grams might say. But anyhow, in tha rest of tha 70's and 80's I swehr I caught that bug six times, and each time he was even biggah. And I knew him from that missin left crushah. So aftah a few years, I told tha guys on my boat and some othah folks in tha harbah. And they told me, "Harry always let that bug go, that's yowah good luck chahm." So ya knawwhat? I did. Caught him a few moh times, aftah that figuh he was too big foh tha trap. Must've been an old fuc- well he was old like me. And ya know, all around that time, my life was pretty good and I stahted ta think that bug was watchin' ovah me"

"So yah' dad calls me up befohe tha surg'ry and asks me how Ah'm doin and I say 'Ayuh, I think Ah'm feelin fine. Hahdtellin' with a surg'ry, but with that bug and all, I think Ah'm gonna be fine.'"

Pa Harry looked down at Bobby and smiled, taking a pull on his old pipe. Bobby took in the smell, and found he didn't mind it so much anymore.

He Knew About the Bomb
@reen58461927

He knew about the bomb. Of course he did. How could he not? The Colombians were always sloppy. He guessed something was up when the usually cold and cruel cartel began cosying up to him. None of his other visits had been like this. He was wined and dined with expensive meals and chauffeurs, which were all much appreciated but still disgustingly transparent. It was that and that he actually caught them talking about killing him. As a true-blooded American he couldn't speak a word of Spanish but even the untrained ear could get the gist when the words *bomba, explosivos,* and *Americano* were all uttered in the same breath.

That morning the deal had gone without a hitch. Ten kilos now for $300,000 and the promise of forty kilos for $1.1 million in a few months. At the airport the Colombians gave him an unusually cheery goodbye but he could see each of them nervously eyeing the briefcase he carried. He entered the bustling airport with the product and his briefcase.

He strolled through the airport flashing the new passport the cartel had given him. The workers who caught a glimpse of his new identity treated him with a sudden respect. Unearned, but as an American he knew he was due it. The Colombians claimed that they'd been hearing words from their man in the DAS that his identity had been compromised and this new passport was a security measure to get him out under a new name. He didn't buy it for one second. He knew the name on the passport. It was one of the aliases of an important cartel member, one who recently had found himself in a fair bit of heat and could do with disappearing. Interestingly ever since he had started taking these trips, he had been told by locals that he shared quite the physical resemblance to this imperilled cartel member.

He retired to the bar where he mulled over the scotch he'd received on the house and wiled away the time before his flight. From his seat he could see out over the runway and to the planes that took off and landed in their constant coming and goings. At the far end of the tarmac, beyond the chain-link fence and barbed-wire, sat a black car. The same one he'd been dropped off in and the one that now contained the bomb they believed was in his briefcase.

Before he got into the trade he'd worked the streets back in New York. Swindling, pickpocketing, conning, that sort of thing. And no other crook in the city had better sleight of hand than him. Before he'd left the hotel that morning the ten kilos he was taking today was presented to him for thorough inspection. Once he was satisfied with the product, he hid four kilos across his person, the final six went into the briefcase, and he was ushered out to the waiting car. He handed over the cash in another plain black briefcase and was helped into his seat by a helpful cartel member who handed him the case of cocaine once he was in his seat. But the briefcase handed back to him was not the same as had been taken just moments before. He'd pulled the same trick many times before. He knew what was up. Act the gentleman, offer to take the mark's bag as they get into a car, and pass them back an identical but empty bag in exchange. The briefcase he had checked over at the hotel was no longer with him and now this new briefcase he had been given was full of something else.

A few minutes later, as the car sat impatiently at a set of traffic lights in the sweltering Colombian summer, the gangster in the back seat of the car got distracted by an argument with the car next to them and the new briefcase could finally be investigated. The top layer was cocaine but beneath that was three bricks of plastic explosives with wires poking out. Before the argument with the neighbouring car was over, the briefcase was shut and he waited patiently in the Latin American sun.

Once they'd arrived at the airport he'd made his own quick switch whilst his companions hadn't been looking. The bomb ladened briefcase was swapped for his original one with the cash. Damn he was good. A voice rang out through the air-conditioned bar from the airport PA system. The 11:28 to Miami was boarding. Finishing his scotch he grabbed his briefcase of cash and headed off to his gate with a confident leisurely stroll.

From his seat on the airplane he could still see the black car at the far end of the runway. They had stuck around to push the button and watch the fireworks. The jet taxied to the runway, powered up its engines, and took off. Just as it left the ground the black car beyond the chain link fence erupted in a sudden fireball. A lady screamed, a baby cried, the cabin crew got on the radio and talked in hushed tones, but the passenger in 6A only smiled and enjoyed the smooth ride home to Miami.

Just a few hours later he lay basking in the Florida sun beside the pool of his Palm Beach villa, sipping on a cocktail made for him by one of the bikini clad beauties that lounged around the pool with him. Soon the cocaine would be making its way up to New York and making him several more millions. He'd embarrassed the Colombians but it was only enough for them to not want to talk about it, not enough for them to stop sending him the product. He was too good for that. He was going to make it stinking rich before he died. Ke knew it. And very soon he'd even know about the SWAT teams suiting up outside his villa.

The Spirit of Summer
@USAAristocrat

Nobody knew where he came from. Every year, for as long as anyone could remember, this strange man, dressed in a Hawaiian shirt and sandals, would stroll into the town when summer first rolled in. He said his name was Joe, but that was a lie, everyone knew that. If you pressed him on it, he would offer you one of his seemingly infinite number of drinks, and 2 hours later you would end up too drunk to remember, though you were sure he told you. All the while he had matched you drink for drink, but he never got more than buzzed.

None of that mattered, though, because he was the most fun to have around. He always got invited to parties, and anytime he showed up, (which was almost guaranteed) you had the best time of your life. One time, Kate dared him to jump from the second story into the pool, and he did a perfect triple backflip into a dive. He then proceeded to drag half the party into having a drinking contest, with the loser getting dunked.

One year, however, a chill came over the town while Joe was drinking with me. Dark clouds rolled over the beach, and I swore the leaves started turning. Joe turned to me and said not to worry, a friend of his had shown up a little early, and he would set things right. He got up, and I saw him walk over to a beautiful woman in a sweater and red dress, who I had never seen before. I couldn't hear what they said, but she gave him a peck on the cheek and walked down the road out of town. Joe came back over, and I asked what had happened.

He said "An old friend came by to talk to me. Said to make sure you all enjoy summer, for autumn is not far away!"

Bad Decisions
@flatearthrespct

Summer's here
And I wanna make clear
That I've got just one condition

It's you and me and the devil makes three
Or I'm gonna make some bad decisions
Or I'm gonna make some bad decisions

If you leave me alone
You might hear on the phone
Or read a front page exposition

That when I get to missing you
I make bad decisions
I make bad decisions

The things I do
When I'm missing you
I make a brand new superstition

I keep acting like I'm bringing you back
By making these bad decisions
By making these bad decisions

I run the roads
And the girls all know
I drive a manual transmission

And that when I get to missing you
I make bad decisions
I make bad decisions

The Dance of the Fae
Robert MacDonald

Taylor sat down next to her aunt to sip coffee and to recover. Her aunt eyed her before speaking,

"How did you sleep?"

"Oh fine, but the kids have been so grumpy this morning, it's like they didn't sleep at all last night. Yet not one of them came to me. Did they bother you Aunt Ann?"

"No dear, I slept soundly, very soundly in fact." She paused thinking this over as her niece spoke again.

"You know, this happened about the same time last year too, that's so odd."

"Oh did it now, hmmm, how very interesting. I believe I now know what is going on."

"What?"

"That will have to wait until tonight, come now, the weeds won't pull themselves among my herbs."

That evening it took forever to get the tired kids to bed with the late sun of the coming summer solstice still peeking through the curtains. Finally Taylor came down to join Ann in the kitchen. She was dressed and wore her jean jacket.

"Ready?"

Taylor nodded and followed her to the far side of the wrap around porch, just around the corner from the back door. They chit chatted, enjoying the cooling breeze and the emerging fireflies as the sun set. Yet her aunt refused to address the subject, she just kept repeating, "you shall see".

Once dark fell, and the stars twinkled down, Taylor felt suddenly very tired.

"Ah" said her aunt, "you feel it, it's time."

Taylor just looked at her for a moment before being startled by the back screen door squeaking open slowly. Her aunt placed a hand on hers, to keep her silent and still. Then they came out walking in bare feet and pajamas, all three of her kids, from 4 to 10, in a line. And it appeared there were small glowing somethings about them.

"Just wait now until they get to the trees" said her aunt in the quietest of whispers. As they disappeared underneath the green boughs, the two women rose slowly and followed in dark, silence.

Through the trees the path went down to a creek, beside which lay a grassy meadow. As they approached they could hear laughter and music. Stopping just inside the woods, they looked out at an amazing scene. Her three children danced in a large circle of mushrooms with many other figures, some tall, slim, and regal. Others short and knobby. Some flew like pixies, others played flutes and some forms of stringed instruments.

She was about to call out and race forward, when, again, her aunt restrained her.

"Let them be, they are in no danger."

"But they could be taken"

"No I have an arrangement with them. They will behave or I will stick them with this" she said pulling her jacket back to reveal a hilt of a sword. "They know better than to mistreat those of my blood."

"But how?"

"Your mother really hasn't told you much has she? She always was ashamed of who she was and tried to pretend it wasn't real. But it is, all and more. And our family and those like us, keep the order.

"If my children are so safe, why are you carrying a sword?"

"Because they are fae and forget the limits of mortals sometimes, so we have to prod their memories a bit to remind them."

"Oh… well…okay then."

She paused thinking, "But it's getting late and.."

"Hush my dear, let them be young. Let them drink of hope and beauty so they never forget the world still contains enchantment. Soon enough it will grow dull and modern for them. Don't fret. After tonight, the solstice will wane"

"You know, I think I remember dancing here."

"You did with all your cousins and before that your mother and I did too."

"Really? Mom did this?"

"Oh yes she loved it. Some wondered if she wasn't half fae herself. She changed though when father wouldn't let her run off with a young elf. She never forgave him for that and then rejected it all. It broke his heart, but she didn't know what she was asking for. Their world isn't kind to mortals"

"I want to join in."

"Sorry dear, this one is just for children and maidens. There are other dances for mothers and crones. I could take you, if you like"

"I think I would like that a lot."

"Good, then maybe we can talk about teaching your children."

"I do homeschool them like you encouraged me too. That ticked mom off."

Her aunt grinned before replying "well that was just the first step. No I mean about what you are and who your people are. Otherwise they will not understand why they see what others don't. And your husband."

Taylor looked startled and said "What about Brian?"

"He is one of us. I don't mean a relative, but of our people. That's why I introduced you too him. He doesn't truly know."

"Is this why he drinks a bit too much and stares off?"

"Yes. I have tried to talk to him about it, but he refuses to acknowledge this. I think something happened to him, but then you can be there with him and he can see he isn't a misfit. I hope he can overcome whatever is holding him back."

"Is this also why he seemed more lost than others in his unit when he came home from Afghanistan?"

"Most likely. Over there I suspect what he saw tied in better with his circumstances. He could shoot the monsters without others looking at him oddly."

Taylor hugged herself as a tear rolled down her cheek.

"I wish you would have told me sooner."

"Me too my love. Our enemies broke the clan system. So much and so many have been lost. But then it all changed. I have only heard rumors, but someone did something. And then last year your babies danced their first solstice and I knew the time was coming."

Ohio Summertime
Nikolaoz

(Chorus)
I like to drink, I like to smoke
I love college football, and jack in my coke
But when that sun shines
That feeling's first in line
There's nothing better
Than Ohio summertime (/Chorus)

Have you ever hurt? Or ever cried?
Or felt so lonely like you wanted to die?
Well I used to lie, beg, borrow, and steal,
And I knew that I shouldn't but I still took the wheel
But then I found salvation when I took bread and wine
And my spirit was light, and my soul it was fine
And that's a little
Like Ohio summertime

(Chrorus)

It smells like grass after a mow
Looks like an old friend you used to know
And it tastes like a T-Bone hot off the grill
And it feels like you feel after eating your fill
And it sounds like a BOMB on the Fourth of July
It's all the good things, it's the answer to why. Yeah it's
Ohio Summertime

(Chorus)

Free Fallin'
Brandon Raby

The sun was almost gone and lightning bugs were starting to appear. Little Annie was running around just as fast as her four year old legs could carry her trying to catch one...without any luck. My wife had just turned on the radio and over the sound of the campfire and occasional laughter of Annie, I hear a song start to play:

"She's a good girl.
Loves her mama.
Loves Jesus,
And America too!"

The words were Tom Petty, but this was a cover. John Mayer, I think? I suddenly felt Grace sit down beside me and lean her head up against my shoulder. We just sat there and watched the campfire burn. Staring into the embers, my mind started to wander back to another summer day many years ago...

I had spent the night at my buddy Tom's house and we were trying to decide what we wanted to do that day. Tom said, "Hey, have you ever been to the rock quarry? I hear they can drive whole dump trucks into it!"

Strangely, the idea of seeing such a massive hole sparked something inside our eleven year old brains.

We HAD to see that hole!

"Wait, isn't it too far away?" I asked.

Tom shrugged and said, "It is 2 or 3 fields past ours. We can tell Granny that we are going to play in the back cow field, and just hop the fence. Easy!"

So, after a quick goodbye to Tom's grandma, we were off on an adventure!

Crossing their pastures were rather uneventful. It passed quickly between dodging cow pies and talking about girls. Before we knew it, we had hopped the fence and ran across the neighbor's fields into a large patch of trees.

"It's on the other side of these trees," Tom said as he led the way. The trees soon gave way to the biggest pile of rocks I'd ever seen. I was about to ask where the hole was when Tom took off sprinting and shouted, "Race you to the top!"

I ran after him like my life depended on it!

Tom almost made it, but slipped halfway up and wound up sliding a quarter of the way back down. I made it to the top of the pile first with Tom right behind me. We stood there on the rocks grinning stupidly and out of breath. When I turned around, my jaw dropped and Tom just smiled.

It was MASSIVE!!!

It was WAY bigger than a football field and so deep we couldn't exactly tell where the bottom was! We dared not push our luck and get much closer. There would be no climbing out if we fell...

Obviously, the first thing we HAD to do was start throwing the biggest rocks we could into it to see what sound it made when it hit. Eventually, we started seeing who could throw rocks the farthest. Chucking rocks one after the other without a care in the world.

It might have been 30 minutes or 3 hours. I don't really know...

Eventually though, the clouds started to gather and the idea of walking home soaking wet made us decide to head home.

But when we made it back to his property, the wind had picked up and the rain had already started. We were three fields from home when we ran into trouble... Miss Trouble to be exact. You see, Miss Trouble was the biggest, meanest cow in their herd. She had even put Tom's grandma in the hospital once! She was the boss and all the other cows (and humans) knew it! The storm had her all worked up and she stood like a giant behemoth intent on not letting us through. We walked back and forth between the fields, and she would move the ENTIRE herd to block our path all while staring us down. We took cover in some underbrush on the edge of the field and resigned ourselves to the fact that we would have to ride out the storm or wait until she lost interest. Having defeated us, she decided to lay down…with the gate behind her in the distance. This cow was taunting us!

Some time passed when suddenly, without saying a word, we glanced at each other and nodded. Tom and I both decided we had had enough!

As soon as she turned her head for a moment, we took off as fast as we could towards the gate! She got up surprisingly fast and before we were halfway across she had already started charging!

I could hear Tom just behind me screaming, "GO, GO!"

I glanced back and I saw her charging full-tilt after us. I vaulted the gate and Tom dove right through the iron bars at the last second! Not 3 steps behind us, Miss Trouble slammed into the gate with an almighty CRASH!!!

But the gate held…Thank God!

When we finally reached the house, we collapsed. As the rain began to subside, we sat in the backyard soaked, exhausted, and full of adrenaline. After Tom and I looked at each other for a moment in silent amazement, we started to laugh.

The sound of laughter brought me back to the present. Annie was running towards me laughing and saying, "Daddy, look!"

I smiled and said, "Good job, Annie!"

She had finally caught a lightning bug and brought it to show me. As she hopped up into my lap, though, she lost it. She seemed disappointed, but a moment later, her mind turned elsewhere. She seemed to take solace in sitting here with Mommy and Daddy by the campfire. The stars were starting to come out and had grabbed her attention.

"Daddy," Annie said looking off into the sky, "This is the best day ever."

I smiled and said, "It sure is, Annie."

As we all sat and watched the lightning bugs dance around the campfire, the music continued to play:

"Now I'm free! Free fallin!
Now I'm free! Free fallin!"

The Beach Bar
@Exonatom

Clint arrived at the beach bar in his Triumph Bonneville motorcycle. He sold the car he had in his hometown to buy it to match the lifestyle he envisioned for himself in a beach town. He was tall and handsome but shy, however he was trying to overcome that. It was the beginning of Summer, so he was wearing shorts with a five-inch inseam to show off the muscles he grew over the winter. Every Friday he and Kyle would meet up here. Clint was early.

The sky was clear like it had been all week. Tourists lined the beaches. The bar was out of the way of the main busy area. As Clint was taking off his helmet an old man's voice called out to him from under a tree.

"Hasn't anyone ever told you those bikes are dangerous?" the old man said.

Clint was caught off guard. "What was that?" he asked.

The old man was sitting alone under the shade of a tree. He was very fat. He was wearing cargo shorts with a Hawaiian shirt and a bucket hat. There was a brown stain going down the left side of his shirt.
"My buddy Jeff served in the Marines for eight years just to come home and get his head ripped off after crashing on one of those."
"I'm sorry to hear that." said Clint.
"Actually, it twisted his whole head around. When they picked up his body, that's when the head fell off. Ripped his arm off too."
"Damn, that's crazy." said Clint.
"Well, does it at least get you pussy?" the old man asked.
Clint blushed. "Excuse me?"
"What? You're not a queer are you?" the old man's Boston accent started to come through. "I'm sure it's probably gotten you a lot of dick, huh?"

Clint stood motionless. He couldn't respond and just looked at the old man.

"It must have, what with your mouth hanging open like that." said the old man. "I bet you could fit at least three cocks in there."
"Who the fuck do you think you are?" Clint asked.
"I'm the kind of guy that looks at you and thinks of a faggot. Well,

are you or aren't you?" The old man stood up from under the tree, picking up his half-finished rum and coke.

"What, are you trying to fuck me or something?" said Clint.

"Go fuck yourself." said the old man.

"Fuck you you old drunk. You're lucky I don't kick your ass right now."

"Buddy," the old man stepped towards Clint. "I wish you'd try."

They both looked hard into each other's eyes. Neither said a word for a few seconds. Clint could see now that the old man had cauliflower ear. Clint's arms began to shake a little and he broke eye contact with the old man.

"Look man." Clint said, regaining his composure. "Get the fuck outta here with this shit. I don't even know who you are. Just leave me alone, ok?"

"Tell me," said the old man. "What are you doing here?"

"I'm just here to have a drink with my friend Kyle."

"Oh my God." said the old man.

"What?"

"You are a faggot, aren't you?"

"Fuck you." Clint left the old man behind.

"Oh my God!" the old man threw his arms up. "Youth is wasted on the young!"

Clint turned back around. "What are you talking about?"

"Look in there." the old man motioned his head towards a woman inside. "Do you see that girl?"

There was a girl sitting alone. She had long black hair that fell down the back of her deeply tanned skin. She wore a black bikini with a linen cover up. From outside Clint could tell she had an athletic figure. In between her sips of a gin and tonic she looked blankly towards the ocean.

"I'm 69 years old and that girl in there is the most beautiful and sexiest woman I've ever seen in my life. You oughta see her when she stands up." said the old man. "Two days ago, I saw her with some guy who left her alone in here crying. Not one fucking guy came up to talk to her. Yesterday and today she's been back here, still alone, and I've seen lots of young guys come in here and not say a damn word to her. Now please tell me, you aren't a queer, are you?"

"No, I'm not." replied Clint. He hadn't looked away yet from the girl.

"You wouldn't rather have sex with your friend Kyle, would ya?"

"Get the fuck out of here."

"Well then I am telling you to go in there and talk to that beauty or I swear to God I will kick your ass right here in front of everyone."

Clint could tell by the old man's face that it really could only be one of those two outcomes. His tense shoulders and face relaxed.

"You really think she wants some guy to talk to?" asked Clint.

"I don't know, who fucking cares? Who wants to be alone at a beach?" the old man said.

"Yeah, you're right." replied Clint. "Thanks."

Clint stepped inside the quiet hut and awkwardly sat next to the girl. After buying her a second drink he learned she was visiting from Nashville. He asked her about what she liked to do there and if she likes country music. Morgan Wallen was playing through the speakers at the bar and she said he was her favorite. She had good memories back home of riding around at night with the windows down while his songs played through the speakers. But at the beach, she said, country music sounds different and makes life seem less serious and more fun. He agreed with her.

"And what did you say your name was?" he asked.

She took a sip from her second drink and then lowered her face down into her hand casually. "Addison." she said, smiling.

The Beer Man
Charles Carroll

     For three summers in a row, I was the beer man. While others at my university were all going into prestigious internships, I would become the working man's most important guy, the Atlas who bore on his shoulders the entire economic system, the guy who in a previous age would have been in charge of logistics for a great general, say like Napoleon or Caesar. I would literally stock beer on shelves for fifteen an hour.

     It wasn't too bad of a job, it did have its moments, but every summer I had hoped to get some kind of internship with both a better pay and that even was relevant to my degree, and I would always end up rejected like the fat kid from a gym class dodgeball team. It probably didn't help that my grades were not the best. Anyway, every summer I would come crawling back to my old work.

     To be more specific, my job title was "merchandiser," which entailed going to various grocery and liquor stores and making sure my brands of beer were fully stocked. For whatever reason, I was always promised a route closer to home, but instead I always got stuck driving an hour out to my stores, sometimes in the middle of nowhere. I also wasn't given a company car, so I would have to use my aging 2011 Chevy Impala. All those hours and miles for sure added wear and tear to it, and I wonder how much of its lifespan I took off of it during that time. We were paid from the moment we left our homes, but weren't paid for the return trip home. It was nice getting paid to drive for an hour to the first store, but not so nice having to drive home for an hour or more from your last store without pay.

     Sure, the money wasn't that good, but my parents helped chipped in for gas, so it wasn't too bad. In reality, all the money I earned went towards lunch and energy drinks since lugging around pallets and cases of beer for up to eight hours a day would take its toll on my body. By lunch time, I would scoff down either Chipotle or McDonald's and wash it down with my second Bang Energy Drink, though by the second or third year I had converted to Reign Energy Drink as my preferred kidney clogger. Kidney stones and heart palpitations build character after all and made me a much more productive employee.

The driving in all actuality was the one of the best parts. Driving for up to an hour on the freeway, window down, blasting Metallica and whatever toilet sounding metal music I had on my playlist, all while enjoying the scenery of the countryside of Michigan on a hot and sunny day really was euphoric. In my young mind, I felt fully free for the first time. Sometimes when I would have to head to the next store, I would take the scenic route, partially to rest up before the next stop, partially to get a little more time added onto my timecard, and mostly to enjoy the summer weather.

The greatest aspect of the job was people-watching. Working in roughly four to five different stores a day, you run into hundreds, if not thousands of people. Most are normies, but you do eventually run into some eccentric characters. Best of all is when you continuously run into them, again and again. One guy I would always run into was an absolute joy to work side-by-side with. His personality was the kind that always radiated joy and would light up any room he walked into. The real funny thing about him was he was never able to remember my face nor my name until I had to reintroduce myself every time. He was another beer merchandiser, but for a different company, so we happened to run into each other almost every day. His memory was probably bad since his company made him work sixty to seventy hour weeks, so I will excuse that. For a while he would affectionately greet me as "Guy," but after a few years of thinking about it, I am pretty sure he called me that because he never could quite figure out my name. Ironically, I never learned his name either. I sometimes wonder how he's doing; hopefully he's retired now like he deserves.

Like all jobs, it also had its downsides. Every shopper sees you as the beer guy, and when you're pulling a pallet of beer onto the floor, they see this as the ripe opportunity to crack a joke. Everyone thinks they are going to be clever, but it's legitimately the same joke: "hey why don't you park that outside, I'm in the red Malibu out front!" Truth be told, it was never funny the first time, and by the tenth time I was looking around for a lead pipe to bash their skulls in until I remembered Kroger has a policy about fighting customers. You can only pretend to chuckle, but deep down you feel a part of yourself fade away. Whenever I see customers in stores today trying their stand-up on a poor merchandiser, I nod at the merchandiser so that they know that I empathize with them. I am not going to bail them out of that situation, but at least they know I am empathetic.

The really absurd part was all the questions about beer, as if I was the beer expert and not an underpaid college student. Normally, customers would come up to me with the most foul sounding names for a beer to ask my thoughts on.

"Excuse me, sir. Do you happen to know anything about this one? It's called Sasquatch Nipple Twister IPA. How do you think it will taste?"

"Like shit."

Man, I miss that job.

Untitled
Aspiring Misanthrope

5:57am.

    I woke up just before my alarm. Same as the last four nights sleep. I waddled over to the toilet, and then to the kitchen for the ritual morning libation. I forgot to snooze the alarm in my quasi-somnambulatory excursion but I let it sound off until I had filled the French press. Almost out of beans, I made a mental note to get more. My doctor had me on a mounting regimen of pills for gout, arthritis, and low blood pressure.

    "Low blood pressure?" I snorted, attempting humor "Could I get pissed at something once a week?"

    "Doesn't work like that Morrison." Doc Alvares was the only person in my life now who I let call me that. I chose him as my PCP because, like me, he was a vet on his own after dealing with a life filled with every manner of horse, bull, chicken, and pig shit. I guzzled the pills with my coffee.

7:48am.

    I parked the car and resigned myself to the day ahead. I tried to tell them. To reason with them. To make them understand that although this was what they wanted, the consequences of continuing down this path would be disastrous. It could have been avoided last year, even just two nights ago, but the Mayor would not hear it. Things change in a small town so quickly. The tender is unchanged from yesterday, which was a small miracle. Snacks shelves and coolers filled. Content, I parked my sagging end on a chair and basked in the last calm moments under the rising sun.

8:43am.

    The crowd was beginning to build up outside the fence. The "pool attendants" were starting to arrive, having to pick their way through the running kids. Five staff, and only one lifeguard among the motley crew of them. I am the only other one, and it was my decision to stay that enabled the pool to remain open this season. Provided I am on duty during business hours. "A key source of revenue for the city!" This was my life for the next 99 days.

Perhaps it was inevitable, bound by some thread of fate that I, mere mortal, never had a hope of plucking. Still, if fate is real and all we have our set roads, and nothing can turn us from them, we owe it to the Power that weaves our lives together to not be dead things in His hands.

8:47am.

"Should we open the gates?"

Ah, Phillip, the awkward one. The "last lifeguard". When he started last season, his pasty white complexion became red as a rose under the summer sun. His twiggy arms jutted out from his near translucent torso at odd angles due to a massive grow spurt. He was 16 then, and while his frame had ceased resembling a screen door on a single hinge, it would take time and a good deal of bulk before he would resemble a man in his prime. Phillip, "the loser" they sneered when they thought I, or he, wasn't listening. The only one who came back from last season. All the others saw what coming down the pike – namely, this exact situation – and decided they were better off taking their chances on the highway. He's been a loyal lieutenant, and has trained the new recruits well. Last year I barely got 10 words out of him. He has come a long way.

8:53am.

"Mr. Morrison...?"

I had trained kids like Phillip before, when I had hope for this world. Why else would I join the Army and stay for 14 years, leave to become a LEO in my hometown, then retire and take a job where none know my name, my history, my burdens? Why else if not to protect my failing hope for my country, my people, myself? To find happiness, contentment, solace? I gave up those pursuits long ago.

8:55.

"Mr. Morrison?"

"Yes Phillip. Open the gates. Prepare the troops." Phillip's ungainly boyish grin beamed bright as I released the corny quip from my mouth. He loved being "second in command", not for any real ability to lead, but just to be a *part of something*. That was what he wanted: mission, purpose, direction. If that's what I could give to this young man, after all those things that had been taken from me, I would do it.

8:58am.

"All right. You all know what to expect. Do your best. I'm right with you."

First day of summer and the newly renamed Martin Luther King Jr. Community Pool and Water Park was open.

Knights of the Golden Circle
Richard Rounds

"The leading pirates were powerful men, acting both out of self interest and in order to support the weak among their own people…At this time such a profession, so far from being regarded as disgraceful, was considered quite honorable."

-Thucydides Paragraph 5

The fleet of speedboats bounded over the open steppes of the Caribbean. The newborn sun's rays shattered in a bloody stained-glass portent of the coming conflict on the horizon. The laughter of the men was barely audible over the humming motors and crashing waves, like chanted psalms in preparation for war. The edenic view of the island washed over the crystalline A10s of Harrison, the leader of the troupe. Clad only in shorts and combat boots, he stroked his mustache contemplating the best place from which to begin the conquest. A map of lagoons, cliffs, and beachheads drew itself in the born-leader's mind, the first map drawn for this land in many decades.

The island, once full of resorts and tourist traps, had become a tropical hell in the last 70 years. What were once trinket-salesman and tour guides had become bug-eyed inbred cannibals, returned to their primal state. Their minds incapable of all but half formed desires, worded only in grunts and clicks. Little was known about their way of life, as all those who had approached this land in recent times were widely believed to have been gruesomely tortured and eaten.

Equal and opposite to the degeneration of the islanders, was the newfound passion in a race of men earlier condemned to endless pencil-pushing. These men overqualified and dissatisfied with the peasant-life of bureaucracy, found their noble blood very much alive after the collapse. And so, after fighting their way to the open sea, the warband sought a fertile island from which to conquer the Caribbean.

The natives must have heard the motors. Harrison saw them gathering on the beachheads and paddling into the water on small rafts, shaking their shields and spears, and waving what few firearms had survived the decay of the jungle over their heads. Harrison looked over the men, women, and children of his tribe. He would not risk their deaths in open conflict with the cannibals. Harrison ordered the other boats to cease their approach, and approached the beachhead with his men alone. He and his men were armed with rifles, but soon gave them up to the indigenous warriors. The natives hooted and hollered as Harrison and his men gave themselves up. The men watched as Harrison and his closest friends disappeared into the jungle, surrounded by the painted cannibals.

Harrison could not keep track of the path they took, as he was too busy ensuring that none of the spears of the cannibals were wielded with the intent to kill him. He was stunned to see a grand white palace before him, hidden in a cove deep within the island. While decayed and covered in overgrown vines, its many storied walls appeared like a caver-covered cliff face before him. Forced up flight after flight of stairs, he was finally pushed onto his knees before a tall cannibal wearing a large feathered headdress, decorated with human teeth and cheekbones. Like a nobler Vercingetorix before a degenerate and bestial Caesar, he awaited the verdict.

The chieftain's servants grabbed his hands and pinned them to the ground. The chieftain drew a large bone knife from his loincloth and strutted around the prisons chanting and grunting. Harrison saw that his men's eyes were full of fear, but he let no emotion emanate from his person. As the chieftain knelt before his hands, he bit his tongue. The chieftain slowly pushed the dull blade through Harrison's little finger, wiggling it where necessary to get through the joint. Harrison's tongue bled nearly as much as the stub. The chieftain waved the finger before his people, each painted warrior tasted it before handing it to the next. When it returned to the chieftain, he swallowed it whole, and a wild look came over his bloodshot eyes. Rubbing his belly, he waved the men away. They were brought to a great bonfire near the bottom of the old resort and bound to trees.

The ritual began. The painted warrior men danced before the women and the flames. The women, wearing only human bone jewelry, returned the pursuit of the warriors with primitive writhing motions. Their shadows and silhouettes were a ghastly performance that struck fear into the hearts of the prisoners but Harrison. Finally, the chieftain came down from his palace in a cloak of human leather, bearing the bone knife, shaking his head dress wildly. Harrison's bonds were cut, and he was led to kneel before the chieftain for the last time.

Harrison lunged at the blade too slowly raised in defense. Caught by surprise, his blade was wrenched from his hand and quickly pressed against his throat. There was no need for words. The savages understood that their chieftain, their high priest, was under grave threat, and they backed away. Harrison pointed at his men, and had their bonds cut. The men ensured that the cannibals dropped their weapons, and then had them gather near the water. Harrison saw that the surprise capture of the chieftain was beginning to lose its effect on the cannibals. They grew restless, the warriors were eyeing their weapons.

Just then, from the left side of the beach, Harrison's warriors spilled into the opening. While there were only two dozen of them, the three hundred unarmed cannibals stood no chance against Harrison's men. The cannibals were slaughtered in the bay, and their bodies were pushed out to sea. Not a single savage on the island was left alive. Harrison could leave no possible threats present in the company of women and children. And so there, in a sea of blood, on a mountain of bones, they made their fortress.

Lights and Shadows in Louisiana's Shallows
@WatchmansRest

Pierre and Jacques, two of the old boys as Cajun as they came, were rocking their porch chairs and watching the lightning bugs show up the Bayou.

The first Coonass spat out his lip of dip. "Dat old lady Brackwood always talkin' sometin' else new dese days, since 'er ol' man up went and died."

"Yeeep. Went and died he did."

"You ain't believe dis 'un, dough. She says she saw sometin' on 'er farm de other night." The man was speaking seriously given the subject mater.

"I 'member de last 'ting she saw was. Aliens. Saw a UFO and went out 'der wit' 'er dogs. Rifle loaded with buckshot in 'er hand. Sho' 'nuff, lights and wind and space engines are a-comin' down on 'er little farm, right next de pond."

"I ain't heard 'dis one," the first speaker remarked.

"Well you're hearing it now if you listen—sho' as a the sky's blue in de daytime, lights and wind and space engines are a-coming to touch down on her land. Was gon' be unforunate for interstellar peace, what wit de dogs and gun and all them such, and the spaceship touches down, and old lady Brackwood is standin' her ground dere like de Fury she is, and she hears a voice all sudden-like come from the spaceship."

"What he tell to her?"

"I tell you what he says: he says, 'ma'am, we're from Fort Polk, and our helicopter has been having technical difficulties. Do you think we could please use your telephone?'"

Both the boys broke to laughing. Apparently, Pierre's brother worked as a mechanic for the fort and confirmed the whole story. They each polished off a can of beer, packed another lip, and paused to watch the lighting bugs and hear the cicadas and the whatcha-call-its and all the other Things that brood in the long dark of the Bayou.

"I tell you what." The one resumed. "Dis oder story I was gone tell you, very different one."

"Okay."

"She heard from her neighbors de oder night—LeBlancs, good Cajun family, reliable folk—she heard dere was sometin' scarin' up de cattle, moving around after night. Big. Black. Smelled real bad, crashing 'round de farm."

"What you think it is? Skunk Ape?"

"You lisin' and you find what I think, okay?"

"Okay."

"Anyway. She's spooked, seein' her man's dead and all, and she locks 'er doors and feeds her dogs real good and keeps dat shotgun loaded by her bedside."

"Same shotgun as for the aliens?

"Same one. She keeps dat shotgun by her bedside, and she's havin' dinner at 'er place, and de cows all start hollerin' real loud-like, and they's runnin' and lowin' and all the rest of it. Now, dese ain't her cows. They belong to some boy Jack who rents de pasture, but she ain't gon' let no cows on her land get ate by some dirty Skunk Ape."

"So you do think it's a Skunk Ape."

"Shut up." He paused, spat, and went back to his story. "Well, she got her gun—she had to go to de bedroom, because she was in de kitchen—and she got her hounds and walked out in de dark. Was dark like dis night's dark, real dark, no moon or none dat, no stars. And the cattle is all quiet now, she can't see 'em none. And she's walking in de pasture, and her little house is far off and the lights are dim out here and she's in the middle of dat big old field she's got. And she smells it. Foul, rotten; smell of flesh decayed and fish gone bad and skunk corpses heated up and come apart. Soon as the smells hits, all her dogs—and dese are big dogs, hunters, you've seen 'em—all run off and hide under deir porch all de way a mile back at de house. She's out dere alone in dat big field wit' dat too-big gun and 'er slippers."

"And now she's wishin' she could run like dose dogs of hers all de way back to bein' under dat porch under dat house, and she's tinkin' dat Jack's cattle ain't her cattle, and how 'er daddy back in de day always told 'er to stay indoors and say 'er prayers when de Old Tings come a-knockin'. And she's wishin' she listened, because now she saw it: 'black shadow' is what she called it. She weren't gon' shoot it, seein' it dere and how big it was. She said she 'felt it,' but nobody did know what she was meaning by dat, because she done run home as fast as 'er little old lady legs could carry her, and she tells that it was slow and methodic-like in following 'er dere."

Here the story stopped. The speaker spat out his dip and packed another lip. The second Cajun broke the ensuing silence with a brief cough. "And what happened?"

"Notin' 'appened. She went home and told all de church ladies 'bout it de next day. De LeBlancs backed 'er up on it."

"So what was it she seen then?"

"Well, 'ere's the part you ain't gone believe. My cousin Frank went down her place today—he's de mailman in dat part of de Parish—and he says 'er whole house is come down. Like a little hurricane rolled right on up de Mississippi and right on over just her house and showed no mercy. Looked like nobody lived dere in years, except she was in town just de oder day. Said Jack's cattle was gone too. No dogs neither."

"And dat's it?"

"Dat's it."

Silence took over. An abiding silence—looming, deep. The sky was gone and so were the lighting bugs and the cicadas and the whatcha-call-its. The creaking of two slow rocking chairs filled the void; something great and slow disturbed the still waters that moved now far off in the marsh.

Summer's Legacy
AV

"(shssh) from staying up late, but you just couldn't stay in bed, we'd be too excited for what the day held.

We started out on bikes - we'd (shssh) that neighborhood looking for something to (shssh) end up at the creek and pass the day swimming. When it'd get dark, we'd go to one of our houses to play video games or (shssh) either stay over or call our parents to pick us up.

(shssh) would visit, or when we had cars of our own, everything revolved around weekends at the beach over in (shssh) We'd scrounge up money the whole week between us...that was around the time Doug had to start watching his siblings more, so he couldn't always (shssh) crummy motel where we barely slept. We'd hit the (shssh) as the sun was up, acting like we owned the place. We'd try to play it cool, to catch even just a glance from some of (shssh) awkward and goofy we must've been.

Of course, nights were the best (shssh) always found where the bonfires were, and we'd sit with the girls we were trying to impress, sometimes making stuff up, but more often than not spilling our hearts for everyone listening. Our wild thoughts and ideas never (shssh) girls, but for us, those nights fed our friendship 'til it burned brighter than (shssh) endless. Hmm? No, I hadn't met your mom yet, that was later.

You never got to have a similar experience since the military moved us so often, but hopefu (shssh) most of the guys…and unfortunately, some of the memories too. But sometimes, I can still feel it, late at night or when (shssh) ing etched into my bones…that feeling of being young and invincible, with the whole summer…no, whole life stretching out before you like (shsshhshhhssh)"

"The audio ends there for now...there're also some pictures, but we've only been able to parse about a third of the data so far."

"That's incredible…I heard it might not be possible after so many years, so this is more than I'd hoped for."

"The disc wasn't too scratched, and it didn't appear to have suffered environmental damage…plus, our proprietary program gives us an edge in reconstructing lost data like this. If you'd like, I can forward everything we have so far to your server."

"Yes, please. And again, thank you so much."

"Dad…who was that on the recording? His voice sounded weird."

"The one speaking was your Great Great Great Grandfather…it sounded strange because that audio was recorded about 60 years ago, with technology that's obsolete now."

"Great great great…"The boys eyes grew distant, but quickly snapped back. "That is OLD. So, they would just record their voice…and that's it?"

"Yep…things like MindDrive only became commercial around the time I was born. That's why your Great Grandfather only has a little bit you can interact with…fortunately, there was still enough there to help find these "CD's"."

"Why did you want them? Was there something important about him?"

"You mean, besides him being the reason we're alive?" he chuckled. "Well, apparently he was…the turning point, you could say, for our family line. He started with nothing but by the end was able to pass on enough to allow our family to begin creating generational wealth. He's the reason why, all these years later, we're able to live somewhere that", he pointed outside, "avoids much of the squabbling and wars that go on down here."

"Huh…so pretty important…"

"Definitely. Y'know, your Grandfather is coming with us on our New Atlantis summer trip…you should ask him about all of this, he'd love it. And maybe…I can bring you to talk to your Great Grandfather via MindDrive?"

The boy looked out his window as they lifted off towards their orbital community – first down, at the city landscape growing smaller underneath them…then up, as the stars started poking through the darkness of space that unfolded itself before them. He turned back to his Dad.

"Sure…I think I'd like that."

Apalachicola
John Slaughter

I could hear the gravel popping as we eased to a stop, the sound of each crunching pebble under the tires marking our arrival. We had finally made it. Four hundred miles from home, from friends, from summer ball, and four hundred miles from Jennifer Mitchell and her C-cups

"We're here." I opened my eyes to find my father leaning over the back seat, shaking my knee.

"Yeah."

"Don't sound so happy."

"Yeah," I repeated, stepping out of the truck and into the salty ocean breeze. What peace the Gulf provided was instantly interrupted by the perpetually drunken figure that was Uncle Ron. He stood with both hands on his hips, his gut hanging low, his long gray hair greased back. His face was unshaven, his left cheek was packed tight with chew, and he wore a tattered black eye patch that concealed an empty socket. As a child, I was told the missing eye was a tragedy of war. But like everything with Uncle Ron, the truth was less honorable, his eye was lost to a rogue fishing hook and too much rum.

"Welcome to paradise," Uncle Ron slurred, through a gap-toothed grin. The cabin behind him somehow looked worse than he did, with its peeling paint and sagging roof. How I was going to spend my summer here I didn't know.

"There's my favorite nephew," Ron said, grabbing me by the back of the neck.

"Yeah," I muttered, shaking my head and pushing his hand away.

Ron turned to my father, "What's his problem?"

"He's got a stick up his ass. He thinks he's missing all the essential sixteen-year-old summer shit."

Ron laughed and spit a stream of tobacco into the dirt and it splashed onto his feet and he wiped them off in the grass. "Must be a girl?"

"That's always a part of it."

"You got a girlfriend?" Ron asked, shielding his eyes from the sun.

"She's not my girlfriend."

"Then why you look so sour?"

I didn't want to answer, but I was tired and irritated, and my words took on a life of their own. "Because I don't want to be here. I had plans—summer ball, the 4th of July at the Millers'. I don't want to spend my summer sitting on your boat taking a bunch of drunk tourists on fishing trips." I could feel the anger in my father's eyes the minute the last words left my mouth, but before he could strike me down, Ron stepped in. "Well, you must have grown some hair on your balls talking like that," he said, " Don't worry, we're gonna see if you're as much of a man as you think." Ron walked to the back of the truck, grabbed my bags, and tossed them to me. "Here. Head out back and down the dock. There's a bunk in the boathouse where you can make yourself at home. If you got any questions, Charlie will take care of you."

In the corner of the boathouse was a cot that looked as if it had been pulled from the dumpster of an army surplus store. It was a sun-faded olive green, and its tightly stretched fabric was frayed at the ends. I tossed my bags to the side and walked back out on the dock, where the blood-orange sun hung over Apalachicola Bay.

"Careful, that railing is loose. You don't want to go swimming with boots on," she warned.

I leaned back and gave the rail a shake, and it rocked back and forth like it was hanging by a thread. When I turned around, I saw her leaning against the doorframe of the boathouse, her sun-bronzed legs glowing against her white cutoff jeans. I did my best not to stare but I couldn't look away. Leaning there in her sunkist skin she was perfect, in the way a dream is perfect, like when you're asked to describe a starry night, and in your design, not a single star is absent, not a cloud threatens the view. "If I fall in are you gonna save me?" I asked doing my best to play cool.

She laughed and shrugged her shoulders and her breast moved full and free under her light blue linen blouse. "You look like you could save yourself," she said, brushing her rustic blonde hair behind her ear.

"If I could I wouldn't be here."

"Then where would you be?"

"Home."

"Where's that?"

"Tennessee."

"You're a long way from home then," she said, as she took a step closer.

"Yeah, well, I'm stuck here all summer," I replied, trying to hide my nerves.

She nodded, her crystal blue eyes watching me closely. "That makes two of us. I've been stuck in this place every summer since I was ten."

"Sam," I said, extending my hand. "Just got in from…."

"Tennessee," she interrupted, shaking my hand gently. "Your uncle told me all about you."

"He did?"

"Yeah, something about baseball and cowboy boots," she said, nudging my boot with her bare foot. "I'm Charlie, by the way."

"Your Charlie?" I ask, surprise written all over my face.

"Were you expecting somebody else?"

"Umm… I assumed Charlie was older and more… of a man."

"No," she said, "Charlie is sixteen… and a girl."

"I can see that. Well, Charlie, Ron said you would show me around?"

"Okay Sam, first rule around here: if something looks like it's about to break, it probably already is."

I nodded, glancing back at the rickety rail. "Got it. Anything else I should know, like do you have a boyfriend?"

She smirked, cutting her eyes like the answer was hidden far on the horizon. "Here," she said, handing me a key. "This is the key to the boathouse, and don't trust the cot in there. I've got a spare hammock you can use."

"Thanks."

"I've got to run to town, but when I get back, I'll show you around," she said, before heading back up the dock.

"Sounds good."

"And Sam," She said looking back over her shoulder, "I don't."

She walked away, her curves framed in sunset orange, and I forgot about everything, about baseball, about friends, about the 4th of July. In that instant, nothing else mattered, and I knew that this summer might be alright after all. It might be the best one yet.

The Long Walk
John Cinder

It was hot. August on Canal Street hot. It smelled like baked pavement, Chinese food, diesel exhaust, and the open sewer. Quintessential New York City. Chinatown, most specifically. Garbage everywhere, just the way I liked it. Kept the price of beef skewers down (God, I hope it was beef). Old, bent grannies and middle-aged men smoking cigarettes like gay triad hoods filled the cracks of the street traffic. I weaved through the crowd, working my way to the bowels of Mott Street. My Shangri-La.

The Chinese Hydra has assholes for heads.

I went through a phase in my youthful independence that took the form of riding the 6 train down to Lafayette and buying bootleg samurai DVDs. Most of the junk Chinatown proffered fascinated me. No other ethnic enclave does charming, meretricious debris quite like the Sick Man of Asia. The movies I was after were hard to find titles on the legitimate market. The Criterion cartel had me over a barrel and they knew it. They loved it. Fucking sickos. For thirteen dollars, Chinatown could give me all the Mifune, Nakadai, Katsu, Ogata, and Chiba I could handle; Criterion had me shelling out over thirty for every lick of the tootsie pop. Fucking sickos. Fuck that owl, too.

I spent hours flipping through the DVD sections. The Sick Men eyed me suspiciously for the first week, but I established myself as a consistent and reliable mark with a terminal case of yellow fever. I squeezed out some unique engagement from them as the occasional crack like, "this one very good," or an empty-eyed nod of vague recognition. I'm sure we all look the same to them, but I'm equally sure they all look the same to each other. That's why they're so cold. Everybody looks like family and stranger. Gosh, I'm going hard on the zipperheads, huh?

Fat and giddy from cheap beef skewers with Kihachi Okamato's Sword of Doom in tow, I hit the roasted pavement and descended through piss wall of humidity into the Lafayette Street Station.

Bing-bong. You kind of go into a Zen state when waiting for the train. Your heart is already in the car, your head is counting the seconds, your ears are trying to differentiate between the faint roar of an oncoming train and the constant howl of the tunnels, and your eyes are looking for those funny, dumbass rats that scurry across the tracks. I've never seen one get cooked by the third rail, but I still live in hope.

About ten seconds into the ride back, the lights flickered, and the train slowed to a stop. The fell voice from the intercom informed us that the station ahead and behind had lost power. We waited. It's not uncommon. At the forty-minute mark, it became uncommon. They de-boarded us and we walked along the track back to Lafayette. Nobody got cooked.

A very odd scene greeted us as we emerged from the underworld. People were everywhere. It was like a drip feed of human bodies. Crowds on Canal Street aren't uncommon, but there's always a flow to the foot traffic. More and more people poured out onto the sidewalk and just started standing around, leaning on buildings, or dead stopped watching a plume of smoke rise from distant Brooklyn. A few squeals popped here and there. This was only two years from 9/11, mind you. We all suspected. We all had that itch. Nobody but the tourists wanted to scratch it.

As I walked, I overheard mummers and conversations.

"No power," some said.

"The lights are out," others commented.

"Their card machine isn't working," the rest of them sang in unison.

I still hadn't realized what was happening. I popped a squat next to a subway staircase to catch my breath. My phone was out of juice. An older girl with the biggest bazooms I'd ever seen sat next to me to catch her breath (presumably from hauling around those giant bazooms). We chatted about what might be happening. I spoke to her in a non-descript Eastern European accent. I don't know why. It's something I did with girls; possibly as a defense mechanism — though nothing would have repelled those torpedoes were she to arm them. I thought about giving her my number, but knew she would laugh and say something like, "Why, so I can give you a ride to school?" I still resent her for that thing she never said. When you're that young, everything is a fantasy. Now that I'm old, they've congealed into hard delusions, which I use to fuel my benders. We parted without incident.

Whenever something big happens, the cabs disappear. The chips are down and everybody eats the fare. I kind of panicked at that point. The buses filled up, and they stopped letting people on. Getting back home from Canal Street was a simple shot up Broadway for 162 blocks. The streets were filling up with people. Cars were getting lost in the crowd. I knew I had to get out of there. With my crispy yellow bag in hand, I set out for 156th Street.

It took me five hours to walk almost the entirety of Manhattan. Thousands of people were in the streets. All the way up to Washington Heights, grocers and restaurants set their perishables out on street tables, marked at fire-sale prices. People were laughing, eating, drinking, high-fiving, and just straight chilling. Nobody rioted. No one got laid out. Only like three people got shot and those were from pre-established beefs. For 162 blocks, everybody was just hanging out. Even the cops directing emergency traffic in the streets had a whimsical smirk on their faces. We would find out that evening that this blackout went from Canada to Southern Pennsylvania.

When I got home, the entire building was having a candlelit dinner together in the lobby. Nobody was worried. Nobody was crying. I helped myself to some lukewarm baked chicken with asparagus, also lukewarm, and found out everyone had similar escapades. The thing I remember most is the laughter. Maybe everyone was exhausted from 9/11. Maybe it was too damn hot. It was the most amicable disaster I'd ever been a part of. It didn't matter that I couldn't watch my DVD. The disc was a blank Memorex, anyway. Fucking sickos.

Women
Thomas Edgemon

The boat is skimming across Mobile Bay. We're in search of a marina with cold beer and marine gas. Dave's father-in-law is driving, taking his role seriously. Dave and I are sitting at the stern, using the live well as a cooler and watching the sun set. The women are at the bow, having to shout at each other to overcome the salty, heavy wind. An oceanic sewing circle. Dave motions at me, and I lean toward him. He points at the women.

"Can you believe this?" He shakes his head and cracks open another Busch Light. "Women..."

Made in the USA
Columbia, SC
26 June 2024